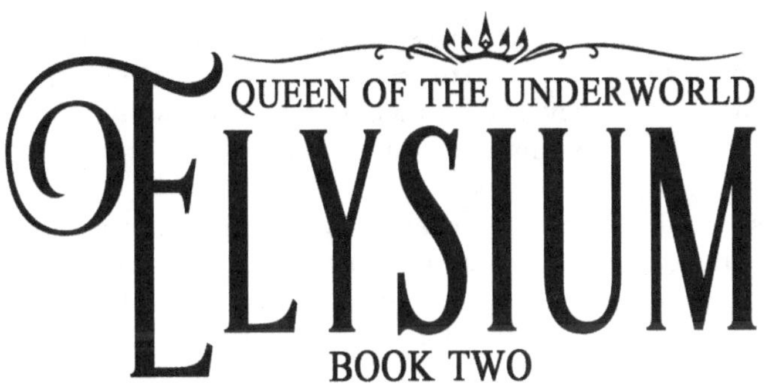

I0725801

QUEEN OF THE UNDERWORLD
ELYSIUM
BOOK TWO

FoxTales Press

DANI HOOTS

CHAPTER 1

Chrys

"What… what do you mean, Father? I saved you. You no longer have to suffer in Tartarus."

His eyes were full of fury and confusion. I watched as he tried to gather himself before speaking to me. I had seen this look before—it was the look that he had when he was about to scold me. He was trying to calm himself so he wouldn't say the wrong thing.

But I had done all this for him. Why couldn't he see that?

"Why did you open the doors to Tartarus?" he finally asked slowly.

"I-I just wanted to see you again. You didn't deserve

this. I had to do something to save you. You shouldn't be in Tartarus for the rest of eternity."

He shook his head. "It doesn't matter what I deserve—what matters is that now all sorts of monsters have been let loose. Now I ask again, what have you done?"

Tears filled my eyes. "I'll put them back, Father, I swear! I'm strong enough!"

"No, daughter, you are not. This is more than just putting some bugs back in a cage. The lock has been opened, and now a new one must be used to seal everything away. Do you have another lock?"

Another lock? I shook my head slowly and whispered, "No."

"I thought not. You have any idea what is going to happen next?"

I shook my head again. I honestly hadn't thought this all the way through. I thought once I got him out of there, I could close the gate again. I guess I was wrong. Panic consumed me. This wasn't how all this was supposed to go—we were supposed to be reunited and everything would be okay after that. As everything that had happened in the last few moments came flooding into my mind, I realized what I had done. I should have waited—I should have consulted with others so that we could come up with a plan to stop Kronos before he escaped. Now we would have to completely start over. It was all my fault. I was going to bring upon the apocalypse.

Before Father said anything more, there was a loud roar. I quickly covered my ears as I felt like the sound was going to burst my eardrums. I glanced up at Father, who didn't even falter. Was this what he heard all the time he was down here? I couldn't imagine what kind of torment this was since it felt as if my ears were going to bleed. I wanted more than anything for it to stop, but it kept on going—as if the roar was the only thing that existed. It was the sound of anger and resentment but also one that saw a taste of freedom. Kronos had realized what had happened and was trying to get away —just like every ghost and creature that was locked down there.

And it was all because of me.

The sound finally stopped, and I glanced around. Only darkness surrounded me. "What was that?"

Father stared out at the darkness. "Kronos. He's gaining his power now that the gates are open, and he's leaving."

My stomach felt as if it were twisting into knots. "I'll

be able to stop him, Father. I swear I will."

He pinched the bridge of his nose. "No. No, you won't. This is the end of the world. We have nothing to stop Kronos. Not anymore."

My mouth opened, but I didn't know how to respond. Was this really the end? No. I wouldn't allow it. I would stop it, just like I always did. I had stopped Zeus and Poseidon, and I would be able to stop Kronos.

There was another roar that shook the entire ground. I went down to my knees and held my hands to my ears again. I wanted to scream with it as the pain shot through my head. The noise was so loud I began to feel dizzy. Why wasn't he leaving? Was he waiting for something? Or was he searching? Suddenly the sound stopped, and I opened my eyes to find another figure with my father.

"This is all your fault, daughter of Hades. If you had simply died, none of this would have happened."

It was Zeus. I rolled my eyes as I stood up. This was not something I needed right now. "And if you had simply let me live my life, none of us would have died and we would be back to the way everything was."

He pointed at me. "No, this is your fault! You should have never been born!"

"Enough!" Father shouted. He took a deep breath, gathering himself. "Zeus, this is honestly your fault. Chrys, stop provoking Zeus."

I mumbled to myself, "He started it."

Father gave me a look, then continued. "First thing's first, where is Poseidon?"

Zeus shrugged. "Beats me. You two are the first souls I have seen in a long time. I've only been able to hear screaming and Kronos now."

Hades nodded. "Same for me. I presume he either got out or is somewhere here in the darkness."

"Only one way to find out." Zeus turned to face the darkness. "Poseidon! You whore! Come here!"

There was only silence. Zeus shrugged. "I guess he's gone."

Hades sighed. "Well, that's somewhat concerning. But nonetheless, we need to get out of here before he sees us."

Zeus agreed. "Yeah, I don't particularly want to face daddy dearest in this setting."

"That's something the two of us can agree on, brother."

"You realize the weapons we used the first time against Kronos are gone, right?" Zeus commented as we began walking toward the gate.

"I do. That's why we are in a bit of a pickle."

"Because of your daughter."

Hades's eyes turned dark as he glared at Zeus. "Don't test my patience. I may not be able to send you to Tartarus, but I can still give you a beating."

Zeus grabbed Hades's shoulder and whirled him around. "Do you really want to fight me, big brother? Because I'll take you out again!"

"Please. You only won because I sacrificed myself for my daughter. If it had only been the two of us, I would have taken you out."

Zeus shoved him. "Then come on! Let's do this now that we have no worry of death!"

I expected my father to ignore his brother's request, but I was wrong. Hades took his suit jacket off and rolled up his sleeves.

"I've waited a long while to knock your teeth out, Zeus. Thank you for giving me this chance."

I folded my arms in front of myself. "Are you two really doing this now? Don't we need to get out of here before Kronos comes this way?"

"It will only be a second before I knock your father out, Chrys. We'll be out of here before Kronos comes."

"You are wrong. I am going to be knocking you out first."

I rolled my eyes and watched as they started swinging at each other. This was the saddest fight in existence. It was apparent that they only normally fought with their powers. I presumed they couldn't use them in here, or they didn't want to alert Kronos where they were.

Father made contact with Zeus's face and shook his hand as if it hurt. Well, I supposed it was good he could feel some pain as that meant his body had been restored. Zeus wiped blood off his lip and then tackled my father. Zeus was able to get a few punches in before my father rolled and got Zeus off him. Father punched him in the face, and more blood spilled from his mouth.

This was pathetic. I couldn't watch this anymore, mainly because at this rate neither of them was going to be able to walk out of here on their own.

"Enough!" I yelled as I used my power to knock them away from each other.

Black currents left my hand and sent them back. I didn't have to worry about them dying because, well, they were dead and apparently nothing got stuck in Tartarus until there was a new lock. Both Father and

Zeus hit the ground and groaned.

"Chrys! What do you think you are doing?" Father yelled.

"Stopping you two from acting like complete idiots!" I yelled back. "You are grown men and you are just bitch-slapping each other! We need to get out of here!"

Zeus shook his head. "No, you foolish child! If you use your power like that, Kronos will sense it and come straight here to devour us all!"

So that was why they weren't using their powers. They should have really mentioned that earlier. Just as I was about to say we needed to run, a loud, explosive roar blasted through the area, sending us backward toward the gate.

CHAPTER 2

Huntley

There was a huge roar, and more darkness came rushing out of Tartarus. It felt as if it were a hurricane coming from gate. I was thrown back several feet and ran straight into Hermes and Pothos, who both let out an oomph as we hit the ground. Maka and Mel threw up a dark barrier around themselves so they weren't thrown back. They were definitely smarter than us and perhaps stronger in a way.

"Please get off me," Pothos groaned.

I rolled off him but not without accidentally kneeing Hermes in the stomach.

"Damn it, Huntley," Hermes remarked, rubbing his

stomach. "Did you really have to do that?"

"Sorry," I said as I turned to the gate that was still releasing such wind and energy. "What is that?"

"It's Kronos. We need to get out of here before the whole of Tartarus blows," Pothos explained.

I shook my head. "No, Chrys is in there! We can't leave her!"

Hermes placed his hand on my shoulder. "She will be all right. She is born of this place. The energy won't hurt her."

"What about Kronos? Won't he attack her?"

Hermes's smile didn't change. "The energy won't hurt her."

"Yeah, I thought as much. What if she doesn't find Hades? And is in there alone fighting Kronos?"

"Then she will be facing the repercussions of her actions. I'm sorry, Huntley, but we need to leave, or we'll all face getting swallowed by that vile creature. She is strong and will be able to fight them on her own. Besides, there wouldn't be anything you could do. You would be in the way."

I knew he was right. I glanced back to the gate and let out a sigh. "Fine. Let's get out of here."

Hermes turned to Maka and Mel. "You two, do you

have a way out of here?"

Mel nodded. "You take those two damsels in distress and get to safety. We'll meet you at the castle."

I wanted to comment on her calling us damsels in distress, but she had a point. Pothos and I had no way to protect ourselves. Pothos quickly hopped on Hermes's back, and I sighed as I would have to be carried like a princess.

Hermes picked me up just as more energy and a roar came out of the gate. Hermes flew as fast as he could into the air before the darkness hit us. I let go of a breath I didn't realize I was holding as I peered down at where we had left. I just prayed that Chrys would make it out of there safely and meet us back at the castle. And, of course, Maka and Mel, but they seemed to be able to handle themselves fine against the energy. Which meant Chrys would be fine, or at least I hoped.

"What happens now?" I asked Hermes. My arms were around his neck and helped support me. I didn't like being this high from the ground without some kind of support.

"Honestly, Huntley, I don't know. I really don't know."

I didn't like how he said that. Hermes usually had all

the ideas possible, but now he appeared full of worry. Were we really not going to make it out of this? Couldn't Chrys put Kronos back in his prison once she got her father out of there?

The fact that Chrys had disappeared inside Tartarus worried me. She wasn't thinking clearly as all she wanted was her father back, no matter the cost. But now that evil—true evil—had been released, I didn't know if any of us were going to make it out alive and whether she was going to be able to put it all back. I wanted more than anything to hold her again and for her to tell me what was going through her head, but I doubted she was thinking this through. Now they all had to pay the price.

Hades's castle was in the center of the underworld. They were deep down in the darkness, but Hermes was flying fast as he ascended toward the castle. It appeared strange now, as it no longer had the waterfall of souls going down into Tartarus. No, it appeared dark all around, as if a calm before the storm filled the entirety of the underworld. I glanced down, which was a mistake and made me uneasy in Hermes's arms, and found that the dark energy was growing more and more. Were we going to get to the castle in time, or was the darkness going to overtake us as well?

I just prayed the others were all right.

"If you can, I would go a little faster," I commented.

"I'm going as fast as I can, carrying two guys. You both need to lose some weight, so next time I save your sorry asses, we can retreat a bit faster."

I laughed a little, even though this wasn't the time to be funny. But Hermes had a point. He was going as fast as he could, and we had been saved by him a few times now. I was very thankful that Hermes was usually on our side and always came to the rescue. If only all the gods were as kind and considerate, then perhaps we wouldn't have as many problems.

"Hermes," I began, "does that mean Zeus has also been released from Tartarus?"

"Yup."

"So if he runs into Chrys…"

"He might be a little mad. Now be quiet. I'm trying to concentrate on getting us to the palace. The barrier around it should keep all the dark energy out."

"And then what?"

"I have no idea. We wait for the others to get back here, but after that, I have no clue. I'm not usually the one who comes up with plans—at least I haven't had to in a very long time."

I stayed silent for the rest of the trip, wondering what we were going to do if we were the only ones who made it out of there. No, Chrys would get her father, and he would come up with a plan for this. He had to.

We landed on the balcony, and all of us stumbled inside, quickly closing the doors. I took in a few deep breaths, trying to calm myself down as the darkness rose into the sky, covering everything.

"Fuck," I whispered. I couldn't even see Oceanus any longer. This was bad. This was very bad.

"I see Chrys opened the gates to Tartarus," a voice commented from behind us. I turned to find Thanatos standing there, his arms behind his back as his brown eyes peered out the window. His white hair was pulled back in a ponytail that contrasted with his dark skin.

Hermes nodded as he stepped up next to him. "She did. Mel and Maka are still out there. Can you see them?"

I didn't understand how Thanatos was going to be able to see them, but he was the god of Death—perhaps whatever this darkness was he could see through it all. Thanatos opened the door, and I anticipated there to be a rush of wind, but there was nothing. Thanatos stepped outside.

"The barrier will keep it out—the balcony included," he commented as he peered below. "Mel and Maka are fine and are making their way up here. There is nothing to worry about those two."

"And Chrys?" I asked as I followed Thanatos, still hesitant that this darkness was going to swallow me whole.

He shook his head. "I don't see her. I'm sorry."

I frowned as we all stepped inside, waiting for the others to arrive. I paced back and forth, praying that she would be all right.

"There's no way I can fly in this. We are stuck here until it clears up," Hermes said as he peered out.

"Will this clear up?" Pothos asked. "There are a lot of souls in Tartarus. It could take a long while."

"It all depends on how many we're looking at in any given moment." Hermes turned to Thanatos. "Do you know how long this will take to stop?"

"I would give it a few hours. They're being released at incredible speed. What I am more worried about is Kronos and what dark aura will accompany him as he leaves."

We all nodded as we stared out the window, waiting

for Mel and Maka as they escaped this devilish wind. I kept pacing as minutes passed. Were they really okay, or had we left them to die? Thanatos said he could see them, but was it possible they got swept away after that? I would have felt responsible if something happened to them since they had come to help me.

After about fifteen minutes, I saw a pair of hands reach up on the balcony. We all rushed outside and helped Mel and Maka over the balcony. They gasped for air as they collapsed on the ground. They were fine, but now the question was, where were Chrys and her father?

CHAPTER 3

Chrys

Shit. Shit. Shit.

The three of us got up as fast as we could and made our way straight toward the gate. There was no more fighting but a simple understanding that we all wanted to make it out of here alive, so to speak. We wouldn't die if Kronos caught us, but we would be in his stomach, and to me death seemed to be better than that.

Darkness covered everything, and it was hard to tell where the gate was, but I had a feeling it was in the opposite direction from where Kronos was coming from. I glanced behind me, and although darkness surrounded us, there was an even darker creature behind us—one that absorbed any light that was left, as if it were darkness itself. But that wasn't right, was it? Wasn't Kronos the titan of harvest? Why did he become something so dark and so rotten?

I turned to what was in front of me. Now was not the time for questions—I would get those soon enough once we were out of here.

Father and Zeus were right beside me as we made our way to the entrance. I could see it now—although covered in shadows, there was some light coming from the doorway. We had made it. I felt victorious even though I knew that might not be the case. Just because we were getting out of here didn't mean Kronos couldn't as well.

We made our way through the doorway and kept running. It was easier to breathe out here, but darkness was pouring out of the gates, making it impossible to tell which way we needed to go. The air was cold—colder than normal, as if this darkness was sucking any life it could out of the air. I peered up and could barely see the tint of blue that was Oceanus. Were these all the souls that were in Tartarus? There were so many.

I felt something grab my hand and found that it was my father. "Hold on, my flower. We are going to be going straight toward the castle as quick as we can."

I nodded as I wrapped my arms around my father. Suddenly I saw dark wings made of shadow grow out of his back, and we went whipping up in the air. I caught a glimpse of Zeus as he cursed at us for leaving him. I stuck my tongue out at him as I could see Kronos as he stepped out of the gate.

"Um, Father…" My voice cracked, my fear apparent. I wanted to scream but was afraid that Kronos might hear and come for me.

"I know. Hold on." His voice was soft, as if he knew how much fear I had inside. I wondered if he was full of the same fear, as he had already been swallowed by Kronos once before. He never spoke of those times, and I really couldn't blame him for it—this was all so terrifying.

We moved faster through the darkness, heading toward the castle. I couldn't tell which way it was, but I knew in my heart we were going the right way. My father had been alive for thousands of years—he knew which way to go.

I held on tight, my heart racing as I could see the dark creature that was Kronos below us. He reached up, and I watched as a hand swiped in the air, barely missing us. I wanted to cry so bad. How was going to the castle going to save us? And had the titan already engulfed Zeus? Not that I really was worried about him —I just realized that perhaps he could have been a good asset to have while fighting this thing. But then we would have to deal with him after the fight. I had mixed feelings about whether I wanted him alive.

Kronos let out a mighty roar again, sending us flying forward. Father tumbled a bit, but he nor I lost our grip. We wouldn't lose each other again—that was a promise I would make with myself. I couldn't lose my father after everything I had sacrificed. Otherwise, then what would this have been for?

I could make out the silhouette of the castle. We were almost there. I wanted to cry as we passed through the barrier and landed on the balcony. I could finally see—I could finally breathe.

"Chrys!" Huntley exclaimed as he ran toward me. He wrapped his arms around me. I began to weep, as I wasn't sure I would ever see him again. "It's okay, Chrys. I'm here."

"Hades," Hermes commented. "I'm glad to see you were able to make it out of there."

I turned to find my father still frowning. I wasn't sure

if he was angry with me or afraid of the titan that was on the other side of the barrier. I watched as the dark wings he used disappeared.

"Yeah, well, I see you didn't stop my daughter from starting the apocalypse."

Before I could say anything, there was a loud bang as a hand appeared from the darkness and slammed onto the barrier. We all let out a scream. Kronos slammed his fist on it again, and the whole entire castle felt as if it were shaking. Any more of this and I thought it might crumble.

The darkness appeared as if it were standing up, its torso blocking out what light was coming through from Oceanus. Glowing eyes stared down at us as the titan began to lift.

"Pathetic creatures. Do you really think you have any chance of stopping me?"

Hades stepped forward. "We took you down once; we'll be able to do it again."

"I look forward to seeing you try—and then swallowing you whole and taking over the world. In the meantime, I'll go after your brothers and sisters and offspring, devouring them all one by one. Say goodbye to everything you once knew."

What had I unleashed? What was this thing? I started shaking, and Huntley held me even tighter. I had made a grave mistake, and now everyone was going to pay.

Kronos laughed again as he grew larger and went up into the sky toward earth with the rest of the souls. I gulped, worried for all the other gods and goddesses he was going to go after.

But they wouldn't be destroyed—they only would be engulfed by him. I could save them. Eventually.

Once he was out of sight and only the darkness of the other souls filled the sky, I turned to my father. "How were you able to fly?"

He shrugged. "I can use magic to create clothing and the like. I can also give myself wings."

There was still so much I needed to learn about our magic. I glanced over to see Mel and Maka standing in the doorway. I ran toward them and embraced them both.

"Thank goodness you two are alive. I'm sorry I did this, but I'll make it right—I swear."

Maka patted my back. "I know you will, Chrys. That's the kind of goddess you are. You just wanted your father back."

I nodded, tears filling my eyes.

"To be honest, I'm not sure you'll defeat him," Mel commented. "But I know you'll give it your best shot."

I let out a snort of a laugh as I peered around to see who else was here. I saw Pothos, Hermes, and Thanatos. I nodded to Hermes, who nodded back. I was glad to see he was here as he was a good asset to have, as I had found over the years. I had a feeling a lot of the other gods in the underworld were fine, since they all had barriers around their homes. The question was simply what gods on earth and Olympus would be able to fight against Kronos.

Then it hit me—my mother was on earth.

My heart sank as I glanced at my father. He was also frowning as he peered up at Oceanus. Was he also thinking of her and what fate might be coming her way? I didn't think that Kronos could be so vast and so strong. If I had known, I wondered if I still would have gone to such measures.

Knowing me, I probably would have.

I was such a fool. I should have known that anything Aether approved was a bad idea. But I would fix it—I had to.

Suddenly, out of nowhere, lightning came crashing from below us and landed on the middle of the balcony.

My eyes felt as if they had been stabbed with ice picks as the light was so bright. After a few moments of my eyes adjusting, I found Zeus standing in the middle of the balcony.

"Ugh," I commented with a sigh.

CHAPTER 4

Huntley

Did Zeus just appear out of nowhere? He turned and glared at Chrys.

"Don't *ugh* me! You two left me there to be swallowed by Kronos!" Zeus yelled.

Yup, it really was him. This was not something I was expecting nor something I wanted to happen. Knowing him, he was going to try to kill Chrys again, but could she even really die when Tartarus was open like it was? Could anything truly die right now? I had no idea how this apocalyptic stuff worked—all I knew was that I was going to hold on to Chrys and never let go.

"You are fine, so it worked out, didn't it?" Hades

commented without even looking at his brother.

Zeus turned his attention on him. "What? Did you leave me there to get revenge on me when you were swallowed by him all those centuries ago? Is that it?"

Hades sighed. "Perhaps. Or I just didn't want to deal with you yelling at me constantly."

"I came back for you, you know! I destroyed Kronos!"

"Yes, and I would have come back for you, so stop your nagging. We need to have clear heads if we are going to try to stop Kronos."

I noted his use of the word *try*. I didn't particularly like that. Did he not believe they would be able to take down Kronos? I glanced around. Were these the only gods that would be left after Kronos ascended to earth and then to Olympus?

"Fine. Whatever. But don't think I'll be quiet once we defeat him," Zeus said as he turned toward the castle. "Now, what do you have to eat? I'm starving."

Hades gestured to the rest of us to enter the castle and head toward the dining hall. I hoped Lucky had some food ready for everyone, as there were just a few more people than normal. I would have hurried to the kitchen to help, but I didn't want to leave Chrys's side. I could feel her shaking still. I couldn't imagine what she had seen while she was in Tartarus and running from Kronos. She had been able to save her father, but it seemed it came at the cost of the world. Not even I thought all this destruction and energy was possible, and I lived in the underworld.

All nine of us made our way to the kitchen. As we almost made it there, I could hear the patter of huge dog feet come barreling down the hallway. Cerberus ran straight toward Hades, nearly knocking him over as he placed his paws on top of Hades's shoulders, licking his face to death. I saw a smile sneak onto Hades's face.

"It's good to see you too, Cerberus."

"He's missed you. Sometimes I hear him whining and find him clawing at your study door," Chrys commented.

Hades nodded. "He's a loyal dog. I'm glad to see he's warming up to Huntley and Hermes."

Chrys smiled a little. "Yeah, he sure is."

Hades kept scratching behind Cerberus's ear. "Even though I trained him to attack Hermes."

Hermes turned around and pointed at Hades. "I knew it!"

Chrys laughed. I was glad to see her smile. It had

been so long.

Zeus sighed. "Hurry up, Hades. I'm hungry."

Hades didn't say anything but moved the dog off of him. "Right. I'll see what the chefs are working on and if there will be enough. If you all could wait in the dining room, that would be great." Hades headed off toward the kitchen.

Chrys nodded. "This way for those who haven't been here."

"I think the only one who hasn't been here, or at least not in quite some time, is Zeus," Hermes commented.

Zeus glanced over at Mel and Pothos, who looked away quickly. "Why have these two been in the underworld?"

"For D&D of course!" Hermes grinned.

"What in Olympus is D&D?" Zeus narrowed his eyes. "Is it some kind of orgy thing?"

Chrys made a disgusted sound. "Not everyone thinks with just their dick."

"Then what is it?" Zeus asked.

Hermes, of course, answered. "It's a role-playing game where you get to pick characters and go on adventures."

Zeus just stared at him. "Because we don't have

enough adventures as gods?”

Hermes shrugged. “There hasn’t been much action until recently on the god front, to be honest. Besides…” He slapped my back. “Huntley is down here all by his lonesome. We had to do something to keep him company, if only every week or so.”

Zeus shook his head. “Whatever. I don’t care at this point.”

We all entered the dining hall and took our seats. Zeus, of course, sat at the head of the table where Hades usually sat. Chrys and I took our seats away from him, and the others filled in some of the gaps. I grabbed Chrys’s hand and squeezed it.

“It will be okay. We all will figure out what to do.”

She slowly nodded. “Yeah, we always do, don’t we?”

After a while, Hades stepped in the room and hesitated when he saw Zeus in his chair. He shook his head, not wanting to deal with him and took a seat on the other end of the table.

“Dinner will be out shortly. In the meantime, I want you all to tell me exactly what has happened here in the past few days, or moments, or however long this took. Starting with my daughter.”

Chrys nodded. “Since your death, I have been

searching for some way to get you back. I have been searching for two years, as that's how long it has been since the day you… both of you… died."

Zeus and Hades exchanged glances. Zeus whispered, "It's only been two years?"

We all nodded.

Hades let out a breath. "Go on."

"I searched through your study again and again, going through all your books and papers, only to find nothing. Then, a week or so ago, I found a piece of paper that was stuck to the back of one of the bookcases and then painted over. I almost didn't see it since it blended in so well."

Hades cursed under his breath.

Zeus slammed his fist on the table. "You told me you destroyed that piece of paper!"

"Quiet! What happened, happened. I didn't think anyone would find it!" Hades turned back to his daughter. "Continue."

"I asked Maka, and she took me to the Fates. They said they couldn't answer either. Themis said the only person who would know is Aether."

Hades stared at her. "Please tell me you didn't visit Aether."

Everyone at the table looked away. Hades rubbed his forehead.

"I was able to get it translated by him. He told me that Hekate held the torches needed to unlock Tartarus."

Zeus laughed. "You listened to Aether? Did it not occur to you that a god such as he wouldn't help without an ulterior motive? That he wanted his children, who are all daimons, free to send the world into chaos in which then he could rule?"

"Which means we not only have to deal with Kronos but Aether as well." Hades rubbed his forehead some more. "Great. Just absolutely fucking great."

Chrys stared down at her hands in her lap. "I'm really sorry. I thought maybe I could close it back up quickly. I thought maybe there would be a way to stop it before it got too out of control."

"You thought wrong. Kronos was not the easiest titan to take down, daughter. It took all of us at the peak of our strength to stop him. Now I fear that most of our brothers and sisters are being swallowed whole as Kronos rampages throughout the worlds."

Chrys didn't say anything but waited for Hades to go on.

"But there is one way to stop him." Hades peered up

at his brother, who was frowning. "A weapon of sorts."

Zeus said, "But we don't know where that is. We don't even know if it's intact."

"I know where it is. The problem isn't finding it but getting to it."

Hermes commented, "You aren't talking about that, are you?"

Hades and Zeus nodded.

I let out a sigh. "Oh my god, just tell us what you are talking about!"

"The Scythe of Kronos," Zeus answered. "The scythe he used to destroy his father, Uranus, and it's the weapon I used to cut up Kronos. I threw it in the sea long ago, and no one has seen it since."

"That's not exactly true," Hades said. "It's at the bottom of the ocean in Amphitrite's domain."

He laughed. "Then it truly is lost. She collects everything that has ever fallen in the sea—it will be impossible to find."

"She is more organized than you give her credit for," Hades said as Luc stepped in with a cart full of food. "But first let's eat. I don't know about you, Zeus, but I am starving."

CHAPTER 5

Chrys

I didn't have much of an appetite after everything that happened, but my father and Zeus sure did eat their share, and then some. I couldn't imagine the hunger they felt from being in Tartarus for two years. I wondered if it was the same hunger that AJ felt after being in the underworld and never eating the entire time he was here.

I still didn't know how he was able to do that, not to mention since the gates to Tartarus were open. He was probably wandering around somewhere. He was not someone I wanted to have to deal with at the moment, not that he could make anything worse than it already was.

Father pat his mouth with his napkin and set it down. "Now, shall we discuss what we are going to do next?"

Zeus was still scarfing down a turkey leg. "Give me a second. I'm still eating."

Hades turned to everyone else. "No harm in starting before you are done. It's not like you'll be an asset to the conversation."

"Hey!" Zeus said, spraying pieces of meat all over the table. I made a disgusted sound and turned back to listen to my father.

"Zeus did, in fact, kill our father with the scythe that Kronos killed his own father with. It was a powerful weapon—one that can split the world into two. It was because of its power that it had to be destroyed. But no matter what we did, it couldn't be damaged. So, instead, Zeus chucked it into the sea like some mad man." Hades gave Zeus a look.

"I did what I did for the gods. Did anyone find it? No. So there—I was successful in hiding it, wasn't I?"

Hades sighed. "The reason it wasn't found was because Amphitrite found it and likes anything shiny and kept it in her collection. No one is brave enough to swim down there and try to take anything from her."

"Amphitrite? As in Poseidon's wife?" I asked with a sigh.

Everyone but Huntley nodded. Why couldn't anything ever be easy? Why couldn't things go our way for once?

"Wait, where is Poseidon?" Huntley asked.

His hand was still in mine, as he was letting me know he was there for me. I loved him for his sincerity but didn't feel I deserved it since I had done all that behind his back. But even then, he wasn't mad—he just wanted to make sure I was safe.

Zeus and Hades both shrugged as Hades answered, "Neither of us saw anyone until the gate was open. Poseidon was either somewhere else or he didn't give a shit and ran off without us."

That seemed about right. He didn't seem to be a team player but was selfish and did whatever he wanted. I hated him with a passion.

"So we need to find Amphitrite and convince her to give us the scythe. Anything else she might have hoarded that we could use?" I asked half sarcastically, half seriously.

Thanatos shrugged. "Perhaps the Shield of Achilles?"

Hades nodded. "Can't hurt. Grab the shield as well. It

is also made adamantine."

Huntley laughed. "Like Wolverine?"

Everyone but Pothos and Mel looked at Huntley with confusion. Pothos and Mel nodded.

"Yeah, what they used for Wolverine was based on Greek mythology," Pothos explained.

"Huh," Huntley said. "I didn't know that."

"Anyway"—Hades gave Huntley a look for interrupting him—"the scythe can cut through anything, so it's a powerful weapon. It will cause great destruction in the wrong hands, so make sure no one else gets it."

I nodded. "Well, it seems I'm also too powerful and can destroy everything, so I didn't think the scythe is going to be too much of a burden."

Hermes tried to hide his chuckle, but everyone heard it. I gave him a little wink as he knew what I was getting at. I was supposed to be more powerful than any god, and yet I needed some large knife to take down Kronos. It didn't make sense, if I were honest.

"Couldn't I just use my power to send Kronos back to Tartarus?"

Hades gestured to Zeus. "Brother, how about you fill in Chrys on how it was fighting our father?"

Zeus set down his turkey leg and held up a finger. "One doesn't simply send Kronos to Tartarus. First, he needs to be extremely weakened, and the best way to do that is with the scythe that can cut through anything. You don't want to use your power as it will lower your power as well. Then, after he's weakened, you need to use all your power and also physically drag him down to Tartarus. Then the gate needs to be quickly locked. I don't know if you noticed this, but since you broke those locks that were never supposed to open, there is currently no lock on the gate."

"Which brings me to the other matter we need to attend to—we need to find Hephaestus to make us a new lock. Does anyone at this table know his whereabouts if he hasn't been swallowed up by Kronos?" Hades asked.

Everyone shook their head. Hermes held up his hand. "I know he's in a volcano somewhere, so odds are that he wasn't captured by Kronos."

"Well, that's a start. Do you know who would know where he is?"

Hermes nodded. "Aphrodite should know. She acts like she doesn't care and couldn't be bothered, but I know she keeps tabs on him."

Hades let out a sigh. "Okay. Here's the plan. Hermes, after it's clear outside, you go to earth and you scout to see what gods you can find and save, specifically Aphrodite. Take them all to the entrance to the underworld, and I'll instruct Charon to let any god in. Then, once you' scouted around, report back here what you see and know. Does that sound like something you can do?"

"Hey, wait a minute!" Zeus said. "Hermes doesn't take orders from you—he is my messenger!"

Hades clutched his fist. "Well then, give him orders."

"Hermes." Zeus turned to him. "Do the plan Hades just said."

Father rubbed his face, frustrated with Zeus. I didn't blame him. We only had been in this room for an hour, and I already wanted to kill him. Again.

"I can do that, sir. Leave it to me."

"Are you sure?" I asked. "You could die."

Hermes smiled. "And we can all die if I don't do something. The entire world might be destroyed if I don't do this, so it's no problem for me. Besides, you'll have to fight Kronos. You need to worry about yourself and start practicing to fight with a scythe. I'm sure Thanatos here can teach you a thing or two about that."

That was true. I had no idea how to fight with a scythe—it wasn't like it was a common weapon. I nodded. "All right. Good luck then."

"I'm not going quite yet, so don't you worry. I'll annoy you for at least another hour or so."

Hades sighed. "I really wish you wouldn't. I'm sure you would be fine going out there now."

"Nah, there are a lot of dead souls that might have some revenge they want to bestow on me. I'll wait a bit for it to clear up."

Before we could continue with the conversation, the dining hall doors opened. Charon came running inside.

"Chrys! Something terrible has happened! The gates to Tartarus have opened!" He peered around and saw my father and Zeus. "Oh, it seems you know."

"Hello, Charon." Hades smiled. "I see you are as quick as ever."

Charon bowed. "Your Majesty, it is an honor to serve you once more."

"Speaking of which, I need you to let any god or goddess into the underworld if they request it. This is a safe haven for the time being."

"Yes, Your Majesty. Once it clears up out there, I'll wait in front of the gate to the underworld. Is there anything else you need?"

Hades shook his head. "No. Feel free to sit and have something to eat."

Charon did just that, and it was a good thing that we were done discussing what our first step was because Charon didn't stop telling story after story after story.

CHAPTER 6

Huntley

It had been a few hours since Hermes left to go find who was still alive and to report back what the damage was to everything. I, per usual, didn't like waiting, but at least this time there were more people with me and I didn't have to wait alone. Pothos, Mel, Maka, and I went into the gym and played some soccer while we waited. Chrys was on the other side of the gym, practicing with a scythe. I kept glancing over, knowing I didn't want to come close to that at all.

Hades and Zeus were probably still in his study, arguing about something or another. I didn't want to get in the middle of their arguments as it seemed like they were always moments away from slitting each other's throat, which really wouldn't get them anywhere. Neither of them could be sent to Tartarus, and I wasn't sure what was going on for the rest of the afterlife worlds. Was Elysium and the Asphodel Fields open? Or were they like Hades's castle and didn't get affected?

The game was boys against girls. We had to teach Maka the game, but after a bit, she got the hang of it. She tied her long blond hair back and transformed into soccer clothes like Pothos and Mel were able to. I sighed as I was still in my jeans and shirt that I had been in for almost an entire day now.

Maka laughed. "Don't worry, Huntley, I can help you with that."

With a snap of her fingers, I was suddenly wearing a soccer jersey and shorts that were a little higher than I liked, but I wasn't going to complain. Pothos and I were both wearing black, and Mel and Maka were wearing white.

"Thank you," I said as I twirled the ball in my hand. "Shall we start?"

I learned quickly I wasn't good at passing or guarding Mel. She scared me still, even though technically I was prince of the underworld and technically her ruler. I didn't doubt that she would be one of those people who fouled and kicked the ball at a player's stomach. I didn't need to be injured on top of everything.

We played for a while, and the girls won five against two, which made for an exciting game. An hour had gone by, and Chrys was still learning how to twirl, slice, and block with the scythe she had been practicing with. Thanatos appeared as scary as ever while he held it, and I could understand how he was the god of death. He, in a sense, was the grim reaper and made sure souls left earth and came to the underworld. I couldn't imagine that was an easy task to partake in.

Chrys, on the other hand, appeared almost natural with the scythe in her hands. She looked badass and was already someone no one wanted to mess with—that made her even scarier.

As we all distracted ourselves, waiting for word from Hermes, Zeus came into the gym.

"I see you all are working hard," he commented as he glanced at the four of us playing soccer.

Mel gave him a look. "We are just keeping busy. We aren't like you, having stupid arguments for hours on end."

Zeus ignored her comment. "The first refugees have arrived. Among them are Persephone and her mother. I figured, Chrys, you would want to go see your mother."

I glanced over to find her jaw tightened. It had been a while since she had seen her mother, and now she would have to explain what she did to cause all this. I was sure Hades was going to fill her in, but Chrys would still have to admit that she went behind people's back and may have begun the apocalypse.

Yeah, that wasn't going to end well.

"Who else is with her?" Pothos asked. "Is Hermes back yet?"

Zeus shook his head. "No. No sign of Aphrodite either. Persephone came with Demeter, Peisy the siren, Dionysius, and Anteros."

Pothos ran past Zeus, heading toward his brother. Chrys followed, not running but walking rather quickly than normal. I followed her, and the rest were right behind, as we all wanted to know what was happening on earth.

When we arrived at the entrance from the docks, Persephone and Hades were in an embrace. Everyone was silent around them, as no one wanted to ruin this moment. Zeus was the last one to enter.

"Give it a rest. There isn't any time for this." Zeus sighed.

Hades glared at Zeus, then turned back to Persephone. "I am glad you are all right. What is going on up there?"

"Up there? First, tell me what happened down here so I can make sense of what is going on."

Chrys stepped forward. "It was me—I opened the gates to Tartarus. I wanted father back but didn't realize the cost. I'm sorry, but now Kronos has escaped and we have to stop him."

Persephone didn't scold her daughter but simply nodded. "All right. That's what I figured had happened. Kronos is rampaging throughout the world. Darkness has filled the skies—diseases sweeping through the countries. Some gods have returned to Olympus to help fight, and others have tried to hide. I was able to bring some; there should be more coming behind us. Kronos was able to get some, including Apollo and Hebe, and..." She glanced over at Pothos who was with his brother. Tears were already in both their eyes. "Eros. And those were the only ones I witnessed. There could be many more."

I felt bad for Pothos. He had lost his brother. They all

were pretty nice dudes—none of them deserved this. I was glad one of them survived, but that didn't mean it didn't suck. I would let him know I was there for him if he needed anything, although I didn't know what I could do at a time like this—a time when the entire world was full of chaos.

Hades tilted his head down so his forehead was touching the top of Persephone. "You did what you could. Hermes should be back with more reinforcements."

She nodded. "He is good at sneaking around. I trust him. But he said he was looking for Aphrodite. Why was that?"

Zeus answered, "We need her to find Hephaestus. She is the only one who may know where he's hiding."

Persephone nodded. "I haven't seen him in some time. I doubt Kronos will find him since he stays out of sight. But as for Aphrodite… I really don't know if she made it."

Hades gestured toward the lounge area. "Please, all of you, come inside and get some rest. I am sure you are all tired."

Demeter, whom I had only met a couple of times, had her lips in a tight line. She shot daggers at Hades as he led everyone inside.

"This is all your fault, Hades! Because of the daughter you hid, now we are facing destruction."

Now, if I were Hades, I would have cussed out this bitch. She was a total Karen—I could just tell. But instead, he gave her a soft smile.

"Good to see you too, Demeter."

She made a *humph* sound and hurried off after Persephone and the others. I stepped over to Chrys and held her hand.

"It's not all your fault. Don't be too hard on yourself."

Chrys shook her head. "No, it's my fault, Huntley. I shouldn't have acted so rash, but I knew if I didn't, there would have been no way to get my father back. I didn't make the right choice, but I'm not sure if I would go back and change that."

I understood what she meant. There were a lot of choices I had made in my human life that I wasn't sure I would change. Sometimes something can seem horrible for a bit, but they might get better. I wondered if this was going to be one of those times.

She turned to me with a smile. "But I'll make it right. Just because they were swallowed by Kronos doesn't mean they're dead. Once I destroy him, I can bring them back, just like Zeus did for his brothers and sisters. Hopefully Hermes comes soon with Aphrodite, and all will be well, and we can find Amphitrite and Hephaestus."

I nodded. "Yeah, I think Hermes will be able to find her. He's good at that. For now, we just have to wait."

She let out a laugh. "Did the impatient Huntley just tell me to wait?"

I shrugged. "What can I say? I have been learning?"

"Well, unfortunately, the more we wait, the more destruction there is. Time is of the essence."

"Yeah, but Hermes knows that too, so he will be trying to get back here as quickly as he can."

She nodded as she glanced out at the docks. "Yeah. I know."

CHAPTER 7

Chrys

I stared out the window by the docks, waiting for more gods to retreat to the castle. Part of me found it ironic that the one place all these gods despised was now the only safe place in all the world. But I didn't say that out loud. I didn't need more arguing than there already was going on.

Mainly from Zeus and my father. They didn't shut up. I wondered what it would have been like if Poseidon were here too. They probably would have both ganged up on my father, as they typically did.

I was very glad I was an only child.

Hours passed and my heart sank more and more.

What if Hermes wasn't able to get out of there alive? What if he had been swallowed up by Kronos and we wouldn't be able to find Hephaestus? Would there be another god to help us? Or make us a lock? I shook my head. I needed to not think about those things at this moment.

I felt a hand on my shoulder. I turned, expecting to find Huntley only to find my mother. She was wrapped up in a blue shawl and watched me with her hazel eyes.

I didn't know what to say to her. Do I apologize? I really didn't want to as I felt, deep down, part of this was still her fault. I had begun to understand her and understand the pressures she dealt with from Olympus, but that didn't mean I had completely forgiven her. She was a horrible mother, but she did all that to keep me safe.

"Have you come to scold me too?" I asked finally.

She shook her head. "No. I came here to tell you I was proud of you. You did something that I could not bring myself to do."

Was I really hearing that right? Was she really complimenting me?

"I may have destroyed the entire world, you know. Started the apocalypse and all that."

"Oh, I know. But that isn't so much your fault as it is Zeus's. If he had just let you stay in the underworld, none of this would have happened. But he has a thick skull, just like the rest of them."

I nodded. She could say that again.

"Where's Huntley?" I asked.

"He's with Pothos—comforting him and his brother. He's a good boy, that Huntley. You are one lucky girl."

"Yeah, I know. But I should have told him what I was doing. I lied to him, and I think he feels slightly responsible for not stopping me."

"Men think they can control us, but they need to learn that they don't know better. You would have done this no matter if he knew or not. By not telling him, you saved having to push him out of the way to open the gate."

She had a point there. What if he did make it in time to stop me? Would I have fought him? I shuddered at the thought.

"I'm sorry I wasn't here after your father died," my mother finally said. "I wanted to give you some room, and after a while, I just didn't know how to approach you. I felt like I would say the wrong thing or do the wrong thing. That was stupid of me—I should have just came."

Tears filled my eyes. "I'm sorry I never reached out either. You had lost the one person you loved."

She wrapped her arms around me, and I did the same to her, my tears dropping down on the cloth on her shoulder.

"It's all right, sweetie. I understand, and I should have come here. But for now, we've got to put that behind us and move forward. We'll stop Kronos, and everything will go back to normal—I promise you."

I nodded. "Thank you, Mother. I needed to hear that."

"Am I interrupting something?" a voice asked, making me whip around to find Hermes standing behind me. With him were Aphrodite and Ares.

Ares appeared beaten, with blood dripping down his forehead and lip. Pieces of his suit were ripped and covered in dirt and blood. Aphrodite appeared shaken, with her hair all frazzled, but she didn't have any wounds that I could tell.

"Ares, are you all right?" Persephone asked as she stepped up to them. "We need to get you to a healer."

He spat out some blood. "I've never been better. I'm ready for more."

Hermes turned to him. "If I hadn't come when I did,

you both would have been dead."

"Dead?" I asked. "You mean swallowed by Kronos?"

They all shook their heads. Aphrodite explained, "No, unfortunately, we do not. Kronos is on earth, devouring everything, but there is a completely different problem in Olympus. Aether has attacked with his sons, and they are winning."

Ares nodded. "Because half the defenses went down to deal with Kronos, he took the chance to attack. Many have given up on fighting Kronos and returned, but many have already been eaten by him. Olympus will fall soon, and Aether will be our new king—until Kronos comes for him, although I'm not sure Kronos wants anything to do with Olympus but just wants to destroy earth."

"Son of a bitch." I bit my lip. So this was why he wanted Kronos to be released—to have the chance to take over. "So we have two enemies to fight now."

Hermes replied, "That we do. I told everyone in Olympus that this was a safe haven, but many wanted to stay and fight. I am not sure what is happening to their souls and if they're going straight to Elysium Fields or if they're just wandering about, but it's a bloodbath."

Ares commented, "Even I told them to retreat, but they didn't listen. Coming down here to strategize is smarter than staying up there. I was surprised when Athena didn't agree."

Persephone motioned down the hall. "Let's all sit and talk. We have much to discuss, and Ares, I don't care what you say, you need to be treated for those wounds."

Ares grunted but followed as we headed toward the lounge area where everyone was gathering who had made it to the underworld. This was the most people I had ever seen in my father's castle. It would have been nice except everyone was saddened because both Kronos and Aether were destroying everything and everyone they loved. I found Huntley sitting next to Pothos, holding his hand. I took a seat next to him and took his other hand.

Father saw Hermes and nodded to him. "Hermes, please report."

Hermes's eyes flickered to both my mother and me. "As I was telling them, Olympus is under attack by Aether. He has taken this disastrous opportunity to make his move on Olympus. Many have already died. I alerted those who were standing about what was going on down here, but none of them wanted to leave

Olympus."

"Because they're idiots," Ares mumbled.

"What of my wife?" Zeus asked, as if he were concerned.

I rolled my eyes. After everything that happened, did he really care about her?

"She is still fighting," Hermes answered. "I have never seen her more vicious in a fight."

Zeus smirked. "That's my girl."

Hades turned to Aphrodite. "We need your assistance. We need help to find your husband Hephaestus. He's the only one who can make a lock strong enough to keep Kronos from leaving Tartarus. Do you know where he is?"

Aphrodite nodded. "I do, but it isn't going to be easy. He's somewhere very remote and inside a volcano."

"We figured as much." Father sighed. "But you know which one?"

"I do. He's in Mount Pinatubo in the Philippines. I can take you there."

"And I'll go with. Kronos is still on the loose there. There's no telling where he might be," Ares added.

"Do you think that's a wise idea?" Hermes asked. "He doesn't particularly like you."

Ares glared at him. "I'm not leaving the woman I love to go out to a place Kronos might be."

Hades nodded to Huntley. "You and Pothos go with them; that's if you both are up to it?"

Huntley glanced to Pothos, who nodded. "Yeah, we can go."

"Great. Now, daughter, you'll travel to Amphitrite's to get the scythe. Peisy and Mel, you accompany her. I presume you two aren't afraid of some scary woman in the ocean?"

Both of them shook their heads. Peisy grinned. "There's nothing scarier than a siren. I think we'll be fine."

"I have loads of dirt on Amphitrite. We'll get what we need," Mel added.

"I'll go too," my mother said. "I'm not leaving my daughter again."

Hades shook his head. "No, I need you here. You can handle all these gods better than I can. They trust you more than they trust me. I need my queen."

Mother frowned, but she knew he was right. Zeus had been keeping Hades occupied by being utterly annoying. Mother was better at ushering everyone. Since she was here, I felt that more of these gods listened to what Father said.

Hermes clapped his hands together. "And I'll go help find gods that need saving. Anyone want to join me? No? Well, all right then. I work better by myself anyway."

I gave Hermes a small smile, and he gave me a wink and headed off. The rest of us gathered into our groups and began our own missions.

CHAPTER 8

Huntley

This was so awkward. First off, Ares was being way overprotective of Aphrodite, keeping his arm around her and all that. I mean, I understood that feeling, as I always wanted to keep Chrys safe even though we always seemed to be apart during something drastic.

Now that I thought about it, why did I need to be on this mission? Why couldn't I be with Chrys? Did Hades trust me enough to know I would get this mission done with quickly? No, that couldn't be it, could it?

"Yeah, that's probably it," Pothos said as we sat in Charon's boat. I jumped a little, as the only voice I had heard for the past thirty minutes was Charon's.

"I told you to stop getting in my head," I said as I elbowed him.

"Sorry, I can't help it. It calms me down. I don't want to be in these two lovebirds' heads, mainly because they might kill me, and then Charon's head is louder than his voice, which is saying something."

He was trying to distract himself. Although reading my head was probably not a good choice, as it was going against his promise to me, I couldn't really blame him at this moment.

"You can play with my mind if you want. I get needing distractions."

He laughed. "Thanks. Yours has always been the most fun."

"Oh? Why is that?"

"You are so rash and passionate. There aren't many people like you. You don't second-guess yourself; you just do it. You do everything for what you love and you never waver. Believe me, that's refreshing compared to most people and gods. Most are selfish, which isn't a bad thing, but it gets boring."

"Thanks, I guess…"

He leaned back. "You're unique. That's a good thing."

"If you say so."

"—and then boom! The entire world turned dark! It was crazy!" Charon went on about Kronos escaping as if we hadn't all seen it.

I glanced forward to Ares, whose skin was turning red. I was rather impressed that he was not yelling at Charon. Perhaps he had more respect for the god than others did. Charon was old, after all, and was giving us a ride. Hermes had taken the three others to earth on his own. I had a feeling he just wanted three girls to wrap themselves around him. I couldn't blame him. I would have wanted to as well.

Pothos smiled. "Don't let Chrys know you are thinking that or the other two, in fact. All three of those girls would kill you without hesitation."

I gave Pothos a look. "Chrys wouldn't kill me; she would just maim me."

"True. But that might be worse in a way. As for the other two, they will torture and then kill."

"I've seen both of them in action. That's definitely true."

Ares turned. "Will you two shut up? It's bad enough having to hear this guy talk."

I peered over at Charon. He didn't even notice Ares's

comment; that was how oblivious he was to everyone. I sighed as I leaned back and peered up at Oceanus. Although the darkness was gone, as all the souls had escaped Tartarus, it was still a bit darker than it was before. I wondered if it had to do with Kronos or because Tartarus was practically broken. I just hoped we would be able to fix it as I missed its beauty—it was almost like a mixture of the sky during the day and all the stars one could see at night, but all a sapphire blue. Now it was a grayish blue and didn't have that sparkle.

It was also eerily quiet, and the air felt as if it were just a few degrees cooler. To many that wouldn't have seemed like much, but when you were somewhere where the temperature never changed, as it was always just a constant feeling, it was odd. It was now just a couple of degrees too cold, and I wished I had grabbed a jacket, but where we were going, I figured I didn't need one. After all, we were headed toward a volcano.

I pushed back my giddiness, as I didn't need Pothos to make a comment. But we were going to a freaking volcano! It was like a little kid's dream come true. As a kid, you hear about scary things like volcanoes and quicksand, but when you grow up, you realize the odds of encountering those, especially in the city, are quite slim. Now I would get to go in one. This was so cool.

Hearing Pothos chuckle made me frown. Damn it, he found out about my childish glee. I couldn't help it though. I had always wanted to see one.

"It's not as fantastic as you think. You'll see."

I wondered what he meant by that, but I presumed since he had been alive for so long, he probably had a run-in quite a few times with volcanoes. I didn't want to imagine what that was like.

We finally made it to the entrance of the underworld. There was a line of gods and goddesses, appearing as if they were refugees of war, huddled together, not sure what to do. It had been centuries, I figured from the history books, since they had dealt with any catastrophic event like this. I wondered if all of them had even been alive since the last big battle or if this was all new to them. I figured there had to have been gods born or created since the last big war with how much they slept around.

The four of us got off the gondola and headed out the entrance, as it was the only place where we could transport, and by we I meant the gods. I wasn't looking forward to getting sick again. Usually now it was just a slight stomachache, but every once in a while I did lose my lunch. I really didn't want to do that again.

As we stepped outside the gate, I couldn't believe my eyes.

The sky was dark, similar to when Zeus threw a tantrum, but this time it felt like darkness. There were fires in the distance as an entire mountainside was burning. I watched as jets flew toward the large, Godzilla-sized creature laughing and smacking them like bugs.

"Oh my god, it's like a movie," I whispered. "But like, this is real…"

Pothos put his hand on me. "We need to go before he notices us."

I nodded, and in an instant we were in front of a lake. The smell of rotten eggs filled my nose. I had expected exploding lava and loud booms and…

Turning, I vomited up the breakfast I had earlier that morning. Damn it, I should have brought ginger or breath mints. After I was done, I sighed. Pothos patted my back.

"Poor Huntley. Neither man nor god. Gets the bad end of both sticks."

I chuckled a little, then straightened up. Ares rolled his eyes.

"Let's not forget when your stealthy character rolled a one and woke an entire cave of yetis and we all almost died," I commented.

"Hey, that was not my fault. The dice were faulty. Hermes rigged them."

Truth be told, he probably did. But I shrugged. Aphrodite shook her head and rolled her eyes as she scanned the area.

"There is a hidden entrance somewhere along this lake. I believe it's that way." She pointed. "But stay out of the water. Some people have had bad reactions."

"I did see the sign, but aren't we either gods or already dead? Shouldn't we be fine?"

Aphrodite shrugged. "Suit yourself. But I'm not going back to the underworld to retrieve your soul."

I glanced at the smelly water. It wasn't as if I wanted to take a swim anyway. I followed Aphrodite as she began to hike around the volcano. I was surprised with Kronos alive that all the volcanoes weren't erupting or something. The sky above was dark like it had been when we first stepped on earth.

It really did feel like the end of the world.

We kept walking, and I did my best to keep up. Although I did tend to have a fast pace, Aphrodite wasn't kidding around. And in heels, which I didn't understand how she could walk around here with those. I guess she really was the goddess of beauty and love.

After about half an hour of walking, she finally stopped in front of a large boulder. "This is the entrance."

I stared at it. It was larger than me. "How are we going to move that?"

Ares shook his head. "Idiot." He stepped right into it and disappeared. I gasped. It was fake? Aphrodite and Pothos stepped through it as well, and I grinned as I stepped into it.

And then I smacked right into the boulder.

"Hey!" I yelled. "That's not cool!"

Pothos stuck his head out. "Sorry about that." He reached out and grabbed my collar.

"No, wait!"

Before I knew it, I disappeared through the boulder.

CHAPTER 9

Chrys

I couldn't believe my eyes when we reached earth.

Mel and I gasped in horror as we saw the darkness cover the sky—an unnatural darkness that made one's hair on the skin stand straight up. Everything felt cold even though we appeared to be in Greece where it should have been warm this time of year. The air and everything felt a lot like my own power, but at even a more drastic level.

Was it because this was my grandfather? Did I possess his same power?

The thought gave me shivers as I tried to turn back to the group. We needed to focus on the task at hand first

—we had to figure out a way to get to the bottom of the ocean.

Hermes pointed to the northwest. "If you go off the shores of Corfu, you should be able to make it there. Mel, you can transport over there, and then Peisy, you can take them under the water. I presume, being a siren and all."

Both of them nodded, and we held hands.

"Good luck, Hermes. I'm counting on you," I said.

He shook his head. "Don't worry about me. Just stay safe. It's up to you to win this now."

A moment later, we were on the most beautiful beach I had ever seen, if it weren't for the dark sky and the waves crashing about. I wanted to come back here eventually, if possible. I had to win to save beautiful places like this.

Turning to Peisy, I said, "You can make it so we can breathe, right?"

She nodded. "But first we need to go under the water. Otherwise it won't work." She stared out at the ocean. "This is going to be a bit of a bumpy ride. Everyone hold on to each other."

I snapped my fingers and a rope appeared. I wrapped and tied it around each of us. "This should help and make it easier to swim with." I snapped my fingers again, changing everyone into swimsuits. I chose black bikinis for both Mel and me and mermaid-styled seashells for Peisy. "And this should make us a bit more comfortable."

Peisy nodded with a smile and turned to the thrashing water. "Well then, hold on."

We all stepped into the water. A wave crashed into me, almost knocking me over to face-plant into the ocean. In front of Mel and me, Peisy dove into the waves. We did the same.

The water felt as if it were going to take us in every direction it wanted. It almost seemed like a whirlwind—demanding us to go deeper and deeper. My eyes were shut—worried that if I opened them, dirt and whatever else this water had mustered up would get into my eyes. Something grabbed my arm and touch my lips.

Right. That was how the sirens did that.

I decided I wasn't going to get anywhere panicking and opened my eyes and took a breath. This was so weird even though it wasn't my first time doing this. I glanced around to find Peisy had moved over to Mel. Mel appeared as frightened as I felt, but after the siren kissed her lips, she stopped thrashing about and opened her eyes. I could tell she was taking her first breath and surprised how easy it was. It was like breathing in air, but we were underwater. I still didn't understand it, but I wasn't going to question it now.

Peisy had turned into her mermaid-like appearance, which was a contrast to her birdlike body that gave her the ability to fly. I had seen both, and I had to admit, this one was a lot more preferable. Her long green tail was beautiful as it swayed back and forth, and her red hair floated perfectly in ocean water.

"Follow me." She turned and started to swim away.

Mel and I did the best to keep up, but I felt the rope tugging me as I wasn't as fast as the mermaid. As we swam deeper and deeper, the water seemed to calm down and there was more and more wildlife swimming around. Colorful fish swam out of the way as Peisy probably scared them. I wasn't sure where sirens were on the totem pole in the ocean, but I had a feeling it was pretty far up.

It was dark down here—much darker than when I fought Poseidon years before. I felt bad that she had lost her sisters that day and was the last siren left—at least that I knew of. But she never complained. She mainly hung out with my mother, however, so perhaps she did complain and I just didn't know. I wanted to do more for her, but I had no idea what that could be.

We kept swimming. Even being a god, my body ached, and I didn't want to keep going, but I pressed on. It wasn't as if I could stop since Peisy was in the lead and she didn't seem like she was going to get tired. I definitely needed to add a pool to the castle once everything was over and swim more. My legs and abs were killing me.

I glanced back at Mel but could barely make her out. With how the rope kept yanking me toward her, I had a feeling she was as tired as I was. I would let her know she could use my pool anytime.

It kept getting darker and darker, and I could barely see anything. I trusted Peisy was taking us in the correct direction and prayed that a shark wouldn't come and eat us all. I didn't know much about oceans as I grew up in the underworld. Some tutors taught me, sure, but that wasn't the same as actually being in it. It was so vast and huge—I felt small and insignificant for the first time in my life.

After a little while of more swimming, I saw a bright light in the distance. I watched as it got larger and larger and realized it was like a enormous bubble of a home.

Was this Amphitrite's home?

With the light illuminating the ocean around it, I gasped at what littered the ocean floor here. There were ships that appeared to range from the Ancient Greek era, the pirate age, and even some modern-looking ships. Schools of fish weaved through the different ships and saw us. They scattered away quickly. I wanted more than anything to run away with them. I wasn't ready to face Amphitrite. She was married to Poseidon after all, and I had sent him to Tartarus. I doubted that she was going to be very happy to see me.

This was a mistake. My father should have come here, not me. Even though I was the one who needed to fight Kronos, as I was the one who let him out, there were better people to talk to her. I didn't even know her —why would she listen to me? We should turn around and the others should go talk to her. Not me.

But time was of the essence—we couldn't turn back now. I wasn't even sure how much time had passed since we started swimming in this water, but I knew that with every second that went by, Kronos destroyed more and more. That's before even mentioning whatever Aether was up to. After I dealt with Kronos, I couldn't wait to deal with him.

He had tricked me. Well, sort of. He didn't make his intentions clear. He acted like he just wanted his children free so he could terrorize humans, not so he could attack Olympus. What would happen when he won and became king? Would he become even more powerful? Other than his drug, I didn't know what else he was capable of. But I had a feeling once I had the scythe, I wouldn't have to worry about him too much. It could cut through anything after all.

One step at a time, I told myself. First we needed to find the scythe.

There were loads of fish traps, planks, broken vases and pots, and other items that littered the area in front of the large orb. If there was even more junk inside, how were we going to even find it? Hopefully she would know where it was.

Peisy stopped in front of the large orb. It appeared like a mix of glass and gelatin as it moved lightly with the water. "We are here."

CHAPTER 10

Huntley

I followed Aphrodite, Ares, and Pothos down the tunnel and into the volcano. It was warm but not as warm as I expected it to be, or perhaps we weren't close enough. Aphrodite made a torch appear, lighting up the area as we went. As we moved farther down the tunnel that was only about two people wide, I tapped on Pothos's shoulder.

"You think this is going to work?"

He shrugged. "Hopefully. I mean, it's the end of the world and all that—he should know to help us. But then again, gods hold grudges, and we aren't the best people to be asking."

Pothos had a good point. I sighed, hoping that Hephaestus would put everything behind him and listen to what we had to say. If he didn't, I might snap.

The farther down we went, the warmer it got, and in the distance I could see a slight glow, illuminating the earthy walls, making them glow like fire. I gulped.

Was I really going to see it? Was I finally going to get to see lava?

We made it around the corner, and before me was like something out of a James Bond movie. There was a large workbench with chairs and tables scattered around. Then, below the rock, was glowing, red and orange lava.

I stared at it, wide-eyed. Oh my gods, it was real. I was standing in the presence of lava, not to mention I was in an actual volcano. This was so cool.

But also hot. Very, very hot. It was like a summer heat wave in Philadelphia and no one had air-conditioning. I just wanted to find a fan and get out of there.

As we entered, a figure turned and faced us. I almost jumped back as the man was large—larger than Ares and a lot more muscular, which was scary. I watched as he glanced between all of us with his good eye, as half his face was disfigured. Now that I took a better look, it seemed he was scarred like part his body was dipped in the magma.

I gulped, hoping that wouldn't happen to me down here. It looked like it hurt.

"What in Hades are you all doing down here?" He glared at the four of us. Crap this was a bad plan.

"Do you not see what is going on outside? Or does only having one eye make you blind to the world around you?" Ares asked with a sneer.

Great, he was going to make it even harder by making snarky comebacks. I rubbed my face as Pothos spoke up.

"Kronos has been released from Tartarus. We need you to make a lock to replace the one that was opened."

Hephaestus laughed. "So, someone finally did it—they opened the gates of Tartarus. What, did they want to release one of the big three or something?"

Pothos nodded. "The daughter of Hades was the one who did it. She wanted her father back."

"Makes sense, she could get around the underworld without trouble. So I take it all of Tartarus has been released."

We all nodded. He let out another laugh. "Well then,

things are probably interesting up top."

I stepped forward. "We need you to make the lock as soon as possible so Chrys can put Kronos back."

He examined me up and down. "Who is this boy? He appears to just be a human."

Ares answered for me. "He is a pathetic human, but he's also the husband of Chrys and the prince of the underworld now."

I wasn't sure how I should take that, but I decided to leave it alone and stand a bit tall. "Right. I'm a prince, and I order you to make this lock for us."

Hephaestus burst out in laugher. He bent forward, holding his stomach as he kept on laughing. I frowned. This wasn't funny. None of this was funny. If it weren't for the fact he was three times my size, I would have punched him. But I didn't need him knocking me straight into the lava. I did not want to find out what that felt like.

"Sorry, that was too funny. You, a human, ordering me around? That's ridiculous. I'm not going to make a lock for some human." He wiped away the tears.

"Then what about Hades?" I asked. "He's in the underworld back where he belongs and needs the lock to secure Kronos once more."

He shrugged. "Then he should have come up here and gotten it himself."

I clutched my hands. Was this guy stupid or something? The world was being destroyed, and he couldn't care less. Pothos placed his hand on my shoulder.

"Just wait. Let Ares handle this. They know how to deal with each other."

I wasn't sure if I believed that, but I would let them hash it all out. It was apparent that Hephaestus wasn't going to take me seriously either way. I crossed my arms and waited for Ares to start arguing.

Aphrodite was being unusually quiet. I wasn't sure what she was thinking, but it seemed as if she were waiting for all this to play out first. For someone who tried to attack us for going in her hotel room, I expected more of a fight. Maybe she was afraid of Hephaestus? Now that I looked at her closely, she seemed to be fidgeting and not looking at Hephaestus in the eyes. If she was afraid of him, why did she choose to come?

I scratched my head. Why were gods so complicated? Then again, humans were just as complicated. That was why I hated being around people. Why didn't people just say what was on their mind? It made no sense to me and always pissed me off. People simply played games and made things a lot harder than they needed to be.

I let out a slow breath. There was no way I was leaving here without Hephaestus making that lock. Ares had better get him to come around.

"Ares," Hephaestus began, "the god who took my wife away from me—why did you think it would be a good idea for you to try to get me to do this task, hmm?"

"Because I know you best. I know no matter who came down here, you wouldn't do what is asked of you. So I decided to come so I could beat you until you gave in."

"Oh? Really? If that's the case, then why don't we skip formalities and get straight to it."

Ares took off his coat, which I didn't understand how he still had it on, and tossed it on the table. "Fine by me."

Pothos let out a sigh as Ares rolled up his shirt sleeves, and Hephaestus took off his leather apron that he had been wearing, revealing tight abs and beige pants. Ares threw the first punch, and Hephaestus easily blocked it and shoved Ares straight back.

Okay, was Ares crazy? This god was bigger than him, which was saying a lot. There was no way that Ares could win this even if he was the god of war, not to mention we were in a freaking volcano. This was not the place to have a fight or else someone might fall into the hot magma below.

"Cheer up, Huntley. If all else fails, we'll get to see a fight of a lifetime." Pothos tried to joke, but it didn't do anything to make me enjoy this moment. This was stupid, and I wanted to yell at them that they were stupid, but I also didn't want their attention pointed at me. I had a feeling they wouldn't take kindly to my interrupting their fight.

Ares tried punching Hephaestus again and again, but Hephaestus simply blocked each attack like it was nothing. Finally Hephaestus took a shot at Ares, sending him flying back.

"Oh damn!" I exclaimed.

"Told you." Pothos snapped his fingers, and popcorn appeared in his hands. He gestured the bag to me, and I took a handful. I was actually getting kind of hungry.

Ares was quick to get back on his feet, but Hephaestus was also quick to attack again. He kicked Ares straight into the stomach, and Ares spat out blood.

Damn, where was Hephaestus when we were fighting Zeus?

It was clear that Ares gave up playing fair as he grabbed the smithing hammer and swung it at Hephaestus, but Hephaestus, for being as large as he was, jumped back quickly. Ares swung again and again, causing Hephaestus to go back toward the lava.

Oh man, was I going to witness someone falling into lava today?

The next time Ares swung, Hephaestus caught the hammer and pulled it out of his hands. I grabbed another handful of popcorn, simply in awe that someone could beat Ares like that. Ares collapsed back just as Hephaestus began to swing the hammer.

"Stop!"

CHAPTER 11

Chrys

We stepped through the gelatin-like substance, and I couldn't believe my eyes. It was like an air pocket under the water, but it also was a lot more clear and beautiful than it had appeared on the outside. There were countless piles of treasure, gold, gems, swords, jewelry—I had never seen so much splendor, and I lived in a castle. Then again, Father didn't care for treasure like this, so most were dark and made of iron or something. I wouldn't mind a few of those though.

This place also appeared larger than it had on the outside, but that could have been from swimming in the dark and not getting a good look at the place. The treasure went on for hundreds of meters until it reached a small castle—like something out of a fairy-tale book. It was taller than it was wide and went all the way to the top of the dome. I gasped in wonder. The trail that led up to it was lined with treasures, and I didn't know if that was on purpose or if there was just so much junk —rich junk—down here that they simply cleared a path so that people could walk through.

I saw why all the gods had called her a hoarder.

"My guess is that Amphitrite is in the castle somewhere, looking down upon all her treasure. So probably up high," Peisy explained.

"Have you been here before?" I asked.

She nodded. "I have. We sirens are both creatures of the sea and sky, so we have spent some time here and helped bring trinkets in exchange for various things. I'm hoping since I have worked for her, she will listen to me."

Well, that was a good sign.

"And if it comes down to it, I can make her see nightmares until she gives in." Mel smiled.

"We should probably not use that tactic, but I also think the two of us need to hang out more," I said. Besides, when I was in London, we didn't hang out too much. I had been so focused on getting my father back I hadn't reached out to anyone to spend time with. I had also been getting used to my father's duties, which took up most of my time.

As we approached the castle, three water nymphs came running out of the castle, swords pulled. Their skin was a bluish tint and almost sparkled. We all raised our hands.

"Whoa, whoa, whoa," Peisy said. "It's me. We came to talk to Amphitrite. Is she here?"

The water nymphs looked at each other. One of them that had a bit of pink mixed with the blue on her skin said, "She's busy right now."

Well, that was odd. What the heck would she be doing right now? I stepped forward.

"I am the daughter of Hades and queen of the underworld, and I command her to speak with me. I need her help in taking down Kronos. She can't refuse."

The nymphs looked at each other again. The one with a greener tint responded this time.

"She wasn't expecting you. Let us talk to her and see if she will allow your presence. Please wait here."

We did as she asked, and one of the nymphs went inside while the other two waited with us. I presumed it was so that they could make sure we didn't sneak in or cause trouble. As we waited, I snapped my fingers and made the ropes disappear. I would just have to summon them later when we left. I snapped my fingers again, and we were back to our old clothes. I was wearing a dark shirt and pants—my typical outfit.

As I peered around, I found that there really wasn't much going on here. I didn't see any other gods, goddesses, or nymphs out and about. I didn't see the scythe mixed in with all the treasures either. I wondered what it looked like, as it was made with adamantine— the same substance as the gates to Tartarus. Down there it had a bit of a silvery-green look to it. I wondered if the scythe would have the same appearance.

After a while, the nymph came back down to where we were. She bowed.

"Right this way, Your Majesty."

I smiled. "Thank you."

They led us into the palace, and I couldn't believe my eyes. The entire place was decorated with a pearl color and more trinkets as far as the eyes could see. There were gold coins, swords, shields, anchors, gems, and whatnots as far as the eyes could see.

What was wrong with this goddess? This was far too

much stuff for clearly one person. I supposed if I were married to Poseidon, I would have gone crazy and needed a hobby too.

We traveled farther and farther up the castle. My legs felt like jelly and I honestly wanted to cry after that swim. I wondered if we could take a nap there before heading out. I had a feeling the answer was no as I didn't see any spare bedrooms, just rooms to collect junk.

Glancing over to Mel, she appeared as tired as I was. I grabbed her hand, and we helped each other up the stairs. Peisy was fine, as she was used to swimming across the ocean. I understood now why Father didn't have Huntley come with us—he would not have lasted as long as we did.

I wondered how he was faring as he had to go into a volcano. I doubted Father would have sent him somewhere dangerous. It would have been cool to see a volcano though. Perhaps later.

We finally made it to the top of the castle, and the nymphs opened a large pearl-colored door. The handles were in the shape of seashells and was quite true to the theme. As the doors opened, brilliant sparkles of shells and rocks filled my vision. I had to use my hand to shield my face.

As my eyes adjusted, I found Amphitrite standing in the middle of the room, wearing a long, flowing light blue dress that was sheer with a solid color tight bodice and shirt underneath. As she moved her arms, the sleeves appeared like jellyfish in the air.

I wanted it in black. I would looked wicked in the underworld, wearing that.

I put the thought of the dress in the back of my mind and smiled as I did a curtsey. "Your Majesty, thank you for letting us come to you in this dire time of need."

"I am happy to meet the queen of the underworld even if she is the one who killed my husband." Her painted blue lips twisted in a wicked grin.

Crap. She did hold a grudge. On the one hand, I couldn't blame her. On the other hand, her husband was a complete and utter asshole and deserved it.

"He was attacking me. I—" I began when Peisy interrupted me.

"I was there, Your Majesty. Poseidon not only attacked Chrys but also killed my two dear sisters. It was a tragic day, and we wish it had a completely different outcome. If there was anything we can do to repay you, I am happy to run errands or retrieve something from the ocean floor for you."

Amphitrite waved her hand. "There is no need, my dear. I don't hold grudges like that. Besides, my husband was a cheating bastard. He deserved what happened."

Peisy seemed to squint her eyes as if suspicious but didn't say anything. "All right, then can we ask for a favor?"

She waved her hand toward the dining table. "How about we sit down and discuss this? Karisa, Delphine, Ismena, please get us some tea and refreshments."

I followed her over to the table, happy to finally be off my feet. By the look of relief on Mel's face, she felt the same. Before we could even begin talking, the three nymphs brought in the tea and refreshments. It was an entire three-tier tray of small sandwiches, pastries, and desserts. It was like an afternoon tea in London. I held back my excitement, as afternoon tea was my favorite meal that I didn't get to indulge in too often with my schedule.

The nymph poured us each a cup of tea. We all thanked her, and Amphitrite finally began talking.

"Now tell me, what did you all come down here to ask me?"

Peisy took a sip of her tea and set it down. "As you might have noticed, Kronos has been released from Tartarus. In order to stop the chaos that's happening on earth and eventually the sea down here, we need the scythe to put him back and restore order."

Amphitrite took another sip of her tea, as if considering it all. Finally she answered, "No."

CHAPTER 12

Huntley

Aphrodite's voice echoed throughout the volcanic chamber. After the sound ended, it was quiet, with only the sound of Pothos's crunching on popcorn and the lava bubbling around. Hephaestus held the hammer up in the air as Aphrodite stood between him and Ares.

Ares looked beaten—like, more so than I had ever seen him—more so than even his character in Dungeons & Dragons. And that included a death saving throw. Blood dripped from his mouth, and his left eye was closed and bruised. I took another handful of popcorn. I had to agree with Pothos; this was quite the show. I just hoped they wouldn't notice us watching like we were. But I was really hungry, and Pothos started it.

Aphrodite stared up at the large man, holding her hand up as if she would be able to stop the hammer. Lucky for her, he didn't swing.

Hephaestus glared at her. "What do you think you are doing?"

"Stopping you from hurting the man I love."

Oh damn. I took another bite of the popcorn, wondering what was going to happen next. Hopefully Aphrodite could deescalate the situation and convince Hephaestus to make the lock. But right now it was as if we were getting front-row seats to a drama.

Hephaestus turned red. "Why do you negate my feelings like that? Why do you expect me to help you when my own wife has left me for another man?"

"Because we never wed out of love! You forced Zeus to make me marry you! Don't you realize that? Ares and I were supposed to be married, and you ruined that for me—you ruined any happiness I could ever have!"

That was a low blow. Pothos smacked me and nodded over to some chairs. My legs were tired, so I followed. They were warm, but they weren't burning my skin like the metal slides did during the summer when I grew up. Whoever thought metal slides in the sun was a good idea needed their brain checked.

"I loved you with all my heart!" Hephaestus shouted.

She shook her head. "No. You loved the idea of me. But this entire time you've been working or hiding or whatnot. You never cared about actually marrying me! You just wanted to fuck me!"

Hephaestus appeared as if he was about to swing the hammer at Aphrodite. I reached out for her. I knew there was nothing I could do to stop Hephaestus from doing, well, anything he wanted, if I were honest. At least not physically.

He calmed down, taking deep breaths, and set the hammer down. "You've no idea how I felt about you. I know that I am a monster—a large, grotesque monster. I just… I don't know. I wanted to believe someone as beautiful as you could love me. I was a fool."

I didn't know whether to feel sorry for him. I mean, he did force her to marry him just because he wanted someone to love him. It wasn't her fault half his body was scarred and he was giant, not to mention I doubted any human would think him that much of a monster. People have physical flaws, and if you couldn't accept that, then you were an asshole. It was as simple as that.

But these were gods, and I had a feeling since all the other gods appeared perfect, I too would be a little self-conscious and feel out of place.

But that didn't mean I would force anyone to marry me.

Aphrodite shook her head. "No, I am not something you can use to fix yourself. And it was never your looks that made me not marry you—it was the way you treated others, like Ares here. You had no problem almost killing him."

Hephaestus pointed at Ares. "He started it!"

"No, you started it a long time ago when you went behind his back to Zeus when you knew we were going to get married. Ares has every right to be angry."

Pothos and I were almost out of popcorn. With a snap of his fingers, Pothos refilled the bag. I took another handful. This was honestly the best popcorn I had ever had. It was perfectly buttered, and none of it was burnt. I would definitely ask where Pothos was materializing it from.

Hephaestus turned to the lava and sighed. "Fine. I'll make the lock. It isn't like I have anything else to do. I'm sorry I have caused so much trouble."

I wasn't sure if he meant for us or for Aphrodite over

all the years. I glanced over to Pothos, and he shrugged.

"I guess that's that then," he whispered.

Standing up, I stepped closer to Hephaestus. "When will you have it ready?"

He nodded over to his workbench. "Lucky for you I already had some adamantine. It will take me a bit of time though, at least a day, if not two. Come back here the day after tomorrow, and I should have it ready."

Aphrodite helped Ares up. Hephaestus kept himself turned away from us as we began to make our way toward the exit. Pothos stood up and threw some more popcorn in his mouth.

"Thank you. Because of you, the world will be saved."

He shook his head. "I don't know what use it is—I'll still be all alone."

"Have you tried going up to Olympus or talking to any other god other than Aphrodite?" I asked. "I mean, aren't there quite a few gods out there?"

Hephaestus shrugged. "I suppose. I haven't really talked to many of them—at least not without them wanting me to make something for them."

So he felt as if he was being used. I could definitely understand that feeling. I stepped forward and patted his back. "How about this? After all is said and done, and Kronos is back in Tartarus, and Aether is defeated and not trying to destroy Olympus, you and I can have a hang-out day. I can see if I can get a few of the others to come, and we just do some stuff, like camping or something."

He turned around and stared down at me. He was at least a foot taller, perhaps two. I was a pip-squeak compared to this god. I bet he could crush me with his fists if he wanted.

And I could see why the other gods kept their distance. It was wrong, as he didn't seem too bad—only lashed out in frustration. But it didn't mean others weren't frightened.

"You mean that?"

I nodded. "I do. I'm sure you all know of some nice places to camp."

He laughed. "I like you. You may be human, but you've got some guts, not to mention are nicer than most. I am glad to have met you, prince of the underworld. I look forward to hanging out later."

"Thank you. I'm glad to have met you. I'll be back to pick up the lock later." I turned and began to head toward the tunnel that everyone else had gone through when Hephaestus called after me.

"Make sure you bring someone with muscle. The lock isn't going to be light."

I called back over my shoulder, "I will!"

With that, I left Hephaestus to get to work and made it back to the others. Ares appeared as if he were about to collapse. Aphrodite was helping him, which I was impressed with because Ares is huge compared to her. Then again, she was rather muscular.

"You feeling all right, Ares?" I asked.

He glared at me. "Want to die right now?"

I shrugged. "I bet I could outrun you this time."

Ares didn't even have the energy to swipe at me. He really was hurting. I glanced around.

"Can we teleport straight to the entrance to the underworld? Or do we have to go back where we came from?"

Aphrodite shook her head. "No, we can do it here. Hold on to me or Pothos."

I nodded and did just that. A moment later, we were back in front of the entrance to the underworld.

CHAPTER 13

Chrys

"What do you mean no?" I asked, almost slamming my teacup down. I watched as Amphitrite glared at me for almost breaking her tea set.

"I don't have any reason to give you the scythe. What is happening on earth isn't my business. Besides, how was he even released?"

I fidgeted with my shirt. "It was me. I released him, trying to get my father back. Zeus had sent him to Tartarus, and it was all my fault."

Amphitrite shrugged. "I don't see how this is my fault. What I have here are my collections—I earned them fair and square. I lost someone special to me, and you didn't see me trying to open the gates to Tartarus. Do you know why? Because I know better. This seems to be your problem, so you can deal with it on your own."

I couldn't believe what I was hearing. Why were the gods so stubborn? "We can bring it back after we are through with it. I mean, Kronos will destroy everything, not to mention Aether is also a threat to all the gods. With the scythe, I can put an end to it all and you can live the rest of your life peacefully with the scythe back in your possession."

She shook her head. "The scythe was something I found myself. It is my pride and joy since it's made of the most beautiful, shimmering green I have ever seen. It was what led me to stay in the ocean and start collecting everything. As centuries have gone by, and the world is in chaos or it is peaceful, I have stayed here admiring everything I possess. I don't have anyone to bother me—none of the gods come here until they have a trade. And that's very rare."

Peisy asked, "What do you want in trade for using the scythe?"

Amphitrite shook her head. "There is nothing. I know that once it's in the daughter of Hades's hands, it will not return to my own, so I do not wish to depart with it. There have to be other ways to destroy Kronos—you just aren't going to be using anything of mine. Go search for some other relic."

Something was off here. She made no sense. Did she really like the scythe that much? I mean, other than it being beautiful like she had said, she didn't have much purpose for a scythe down here—especially one that could destroy anything it touches.

Which might be why she didn't think we would give it back. But it didn't seem she cared to fight ever or leave this place. What was her deal?

If it was indeed beautiful, I could imagine she would just keep it around, seeing all the junk she possessed—but in that line of thinking, she had so many other things, why would the scythe be the one thing she wouldn't part with?

"What about the shield of Achilles?" I asked. "Would you be willing to part with that?"

She sipped her drink for a moment, then nodded. "That I'll be willing to give to you. It's worn and dented. I don't have much use for it." She turned to the nymphs. "Bring us the shield."

Two of the nymphs nodded and ran off to the other

room. I wondered if they would have to search all the rooms or if they had the contents of this palace memorized. I couldn't imagine that being easy.

"Now." Amphitrite picked up the teapot. "Would you like another cup of tea?"

I nodded, and she poured us each more tea. Mel hadn't said anything, but she seemed to have a bit of a confused look on her face. I leaned over to her.

"What is it?" I asked.

"Something seems off. I can see her fears and nightmares, and one of them seems like it shouldn't be possible."

"Oh? What is it? Maybe we could use it to our advantage."

"Well… she's afraid of losing Poseidon."

I furrowed my brows. "But she already lost Poseidon."

"That's what I was thinking. But it isn't an old worry; it's a new one. I'm not sure how to explain it."

I sat back up and smiled at Amphitrite. Was it possible that Poseidon was here and that was why she wasn't going to give us the scythe? Because she didn't want Kronos and Tartarus destroyed? Because then she would lose Poseidon? I bit my lip. If that was true, then would my father also have to return to Tartarus?

That wasn't something I was willing to let happen—at least not without a fight. But if I brought it up, and she was hiding him, it would make her even angrier with me.

After a few minutes of silently eating snacks and sipping tea, the nymphs brought in the shield. It was large—about a meter in length with designs carved around it. The nymph handed it to me.

"Thank you," I said as I examined it closer. The center appeared to have the earth, sea, moon, stars, and sun. Around that were many figures standing around looking joyful. Then around that were figures fighting with swords and shields. On the very edge were more people happy. It was stunning, but I couldn't understand why it was on a shield—a shield that would have been used in war and not just to decorate. Whatever, it didn't matter—it was strong and that was all I needed.

Well, that and the scythe.

"I am sorry I can't give you the scythe, but I simply can't part with it. You do understand, don't you?" Amphitrite said.

I understood she was selfish. I nodded. "Of course. I am thankful I'll have at least this shield to keep me from dying as I risk my life to save the world."

Before Amphitrite could comment, a figure stepped from the back room. I recognized the dark curly hair— it was Poseidon.

And he was nude.

"Amphitrite, when are you going to come back to bed — Oh." He noticed us there and grinned. "Ladies."

I held up the shield to literally shield my eyes. I did not want to look at that. Peisy and Mel, on the other hand, didn't look away.

"Poseidon! I told you to stay in bed!"

"I got bored."

"You know that no one can see you or else they will send you back!" Amphitrite's face was red now, and she yelled at her husband. So Mel was right—that was her fear with the scythe.

"Amphitrite," I began, "I am not here to put your husband back in Tartarus. I am here for the scythe. I won't make it, so he or my father and maybe Zeus have to go back. I'll do everything in my power to stop that from happening."

She shook her head. "No! There is no way you can return Tartarus into its original form with Kronos in it, without their souls going back. It's impossible!"

I felt my heart sink into my stomach. Was that true? "How would you know? This has never happened before. I'll make sure your husband is safe. Just give us the scythe."

"Never! I'll never let you win against Kronos!"

I let out a sigh. "If I don't stop Kronos, he will destroy everything. You realize that, don't you? He will come down here and destroy all this. And perhaps he will take the scythe and destroy everything in existence. And if he doesn't, Aether will. Either way, we are all screwed. You get that, right? If you help me, you'll get a chance to be with the person you love."

"No. You can't promise me that. No, if I don't help you, then if he's taken away from me, I can go with him, whether it be Aether murdering us or Kronos swallowing us whole. I don't care, but I know I'll be with him. You can't guarantee me that—you can't promise me that my husband won't go to Tartarus for an eternity without me."

Well, I had to admit, she had a point there. I really couldn't promise that. I would try my hardest, I swore, as I couldn't let my father go back to Tartarus—not without how he and Zeus described it. He didn't deserve it.

"Get out!" she yelled at us. "All of you! You are no longer wanted here. Leave before I decide to get rid of you myself."

We all stood up and got out of there as quickly as we could. The three nymphs followed us out.

CHAPTER 14

Huntley

The world appeared even more disastrous.

I stared out at the world as it was slowly being destroyed by Kronos as he went on a rampage. Fires engulfed everything around us. I had never seen anything so terrifying—and I had seen Ares lose a board game.

Pothos patted my back. "It will be okay. We'll stop this. But we've got to get into the underworld. Come on."

I nodded and turned back to the rest of them. Ares was still injured and limping—more than he had when he fought against Aether to protect Aphrodite. Maka would be able to heal him and he would be the good old, strong Ares that he always was.

We stepped inside the doors, and as they closed, I felt a bit of relief. We were home and almost to the place of protection. There were many gods lined up and other creatures such as nymphs and the like. I hadn't seen many, as I didn't see much of anyone in the underworld, so I couldn't help but stare at them for a moment or two. Pothos nudged me, and I moved my gaze over to some nice-looking rocks.

"We are able to cut this line, you know. You are the prince of the underworld after all," Pothos commented.

I nodded. "Right." I started forward. "Excuse me! Prince of the underworld coming through! We need to get back so we can save the world and whatnot."

Everyone stared at the four of us as we made our way through. I heard murmurs as we went to the front.

"Prince of the underworld? That punk human?"

"What was Hades thinking letting a human like that marry his daughter?"

"I bet he's lying."

"That can't be right."

I ignored them. I was used to talk like that, so it shouldn't have bothered me. But part of me felt a little bad. I was doing everything I could to save all of them, and those were the comments I got? I hated it.

We made it to the front of the line and found that Charon wasn't back yet. I figured as much since I couldn't hear him. As we waited, the whispers continued.

"Hades must have lost his mind."

"Was Chrys forced into marriage? Did he have something over her?"

"Did he defeat some minotaur or something? He doesn't appear to be a demigod."

I folded my arms. This was ridiculous. I didn't want to hear any more of it. I couldn't wait to be back in my room and just sleep for a day and a half and then go get the lock. I had a feeling that wasn't going to happen, however. I was probably going to be pulling a few all-nighters since I was dead and didn't technically need sleep. It just sort of passed the time and helped me calm down a bit. And I was used to sleeping somewhat.

As the whispers continued, Pothos leaped up on a wooden platform and turned to them all.

"Are you all idiots? Do you get your pleasures by being assholes? This here is your prince—the prince who will be there when you get to your safe haven in the underworld. He saved the world already and will be doing so again after we get the lock back to seal up Tartarus. Do you know of any god who has stepped up to save the day like this human? No? Then bugger off!"

Pothos jumped down from the platform. Everyone was silent, including me.

"Was that necessary?" I asked.

He shrugged. "They were pissing me off, so yes."

I rolled my eyes but was thankful I had friends like him who were willing to stand up for me now. I definitely didn't have any of those when I was growing up.

Charon finally showed, singing some song I had never heard of. I sighed, as I knew this would be a long ride, but it was better than being out where Kronos was. As he drew closer, Charon began to count how many gods there were.

"Twenty-five! Then I need about... five boats."

With a snap of his fingers, four more boats appeared. I widened my eyes. Since when could he do that? I guess we had never had to travel where he was leading the souls before, as these were all gods and other mythical creatures that needed to go to the castle.

Ares, Pothos, Aphrodite, and I got into the front boat,

which I realized was a mistake. We could have gotten in the back one and not had to hear him talking. I sighed as the boat started moving and Charon started speaking.

It would be one thing if he actually listened to what we had to say, but he didn't. He simply kept talking over whoever else was talking. It was a one-sided conversation.

"So, were you able to get the big scary Hephaestus to make the lock for us?"

Oh, it was actually a question aimed toward us. "Ye —"

"You know, a long time ago…"

I rolled my eyes. I should have figured.

"Hephaestus was cast out of Olympus for his hideousness. To seek revenge he made a golden throne that Hera saw and adored, and the gods drugged him with wine and convinced him to bring it to Olympus."

Okay, that was horrible. I mean, truly horrible. I could understand why he was so angry all the time and why he hated all the gods.

Pothos leaned over to me. "Before you get too sympathetic for Hephaestus, he also set a trap for Ares and Aphrodite while they were having sex and dragged them both to Olympus so everyone would see them nude together."

Before I could remark on that, Ares turned around and glared at Pothos with his one good eye.

Pothos shrugged. "He needed to know."

Ares didn't say anything but turned to face forward. I leaned close to Pothos so Ares couldn't hear.

"That sounded like a really embarrassing event," I whispered.

"Oh, it was," Pothos said. "I had never seen Ares so pissed. It was bad. I thought that was going to be the end of Olympus itself."

"I can imagine."

Ares spun around and grabbed the two of us by the collars of our shirts. I was surprised he still had enough strength left.

"How about you two shut up or I'll throw you over this boat and you can swim to the castle?"

Aphrodite touched his arm. "Honey, please. They're just kids."

He narrowed his eye at us. "Shut. Up."

With that he let us go, and I fell back to the seat with a thud as did Pothos. We glanced at each other but didn't say anything. We knew better than to piss off Ares any more at this point.

Charon, however, kept talking, but Ares knew better than to bite off the head of the person guiding the boat. It was another hour before we reached Hades's castle. I could hear some of the gods that were in the boat behind us mocking it, saying it was so Gothic and emo. To be fair, it was, but were they really making remarks about a place that was their only safe haven? I wanted to slap them, but I knew better than to slap a god.

We arrived at the dock, and Hades was there to greet us and show the gods where they could go. When he saw us, he smiled a little.

"You all are back." He glanced over to Ares. "I take it Hephaestus took out some of his frustrations on Ares again?"

I nodded. "But Aphrodite was able to convince him to make the lock."

"Good. Are you all right? There is blood all over your shirt."

I glanced down. Sure enough, Ares had gotten his blood all over me. "I'm fine. Ares got a little mad at Pothos and me on the way back. It's his blood."

"Per the norm." He turned to Ares. "You need medical attention. Maka is in the secondary lounge area taking care of any gods that come injured. Let me take you to her."

Hades started to lead Aphrodite and Ares when I called out after him. "Wait, is Chrys back yet?"

He shook his head. "Not yet. Take these other gods to the waiting area. There are snacks and tea."

I nodded and turned to everyone. "All right, follow me."

CHAPTER 15

Chrys

As we descended the stairs of the castle, I swore I could hear a voice calling me. It was deep and dark-sounding —almost like the voice I had heard when I was falling into Tartarus. It made me shudder as none of the words made sense. Was this the primordial language that the note had been written in? I wasn't sure, but I knew I couldn't ignore it.

I tried to focus, but none of it made sense. As we kept going down the stairs, it felt as if it was surrounding me. It got louder and louder, and I feared maybe Kronos had made his way down here, also looking for his scythe.

Unless, perhaps, it was the scythe itself.

I glanced around but didn't see any sign of it as we were still in the stairwell. There was nothing there but gems and coins and the random small statue. But I kept glancing around just to make sure.

Mel leaned in toward me. "What's wrong?"

"The scythe," I whispered so that the nymphs couldn't hear me. "I can hear it. I think it's nearby and trying to call for me. Be on the lookout for it."

She nodded and leaned into Peisy to tell her the same. As we finally descended all the way down to the main level, we stepped outside to find the same stacks upon stacks of treasure to greet us.

There was no way we could find this on our own. I let out a sigh as I peered around. There was just so much gold and so many gems. Nothing stood out because it all looked so grand. I clutched the shield. While it was helpful, I knew it wouldn't be enough. We needed that scythe to restore order. We had to find it.

I was hoping once we left the palace itself, the nymphs would leave us alone. It appeared that wasn't going to be the case. They were going to make sure we exited this place.

Which made me believe perhaps it was out here

somewhere. Otherwise they didn't have anything to fear.

The voice was getting louder—so loud that I could barely think. And none of it made sense, which was the worst part. What did they want? Why couldn't they translate for me? I knew, after all this was over, I would learn primordial in case anything like this happened again. One could never be too careful, especially if one lived for thousands of years.

I scanned the area, looking for anything that sparkled a grayish green like the gates of Tartarus. I didn't see anything but brightly colored gems and gold. There were statues upon statues as well, and I wondered if some had been made by Medusa as the faces appeared frightened.

"*There!*" the voice yelled in my head.

Finally a language I understood. I glanced up to find the scythe, longer than I was tall, laying on top of a golden pile.

And it was far off—at least a few hundred meters. And we were headed in the opposite direction. Of course.

I swore it wasn't there earlier. I would have noticed it. Whatever, it didn't matter now. We had to get it.

So what was I going to do? Take out the nymphs? I could just… make them pass out or something, but my power could be dangerous if it wasn't under control.

No, I had training for the past two years—I was in control of my powers now. At least I thought so.

Peisy tapped my shoulder. "I see it. I'll take them out. Run straight for it and meet us at the entrance."

Mel grabbed the shield. "I'll take this so your hands are free."

I nodded, and moments later I heard the loudest scream I had ever heard. I knew if Peisy had been facing me, my eardrums would have burst. I was definitely glad she was on my team.

Running as fast as I could, I went straight for the scythe. The voice disappeared as I now had the intention of grabbing it and taking it with me.

Thanks, strange voice, I couldn't have done this without you.

Apparently Amphitrite didn't trust her nymphs, as I could hear her call from a window above. "Guards! Seize them! How did the scythe get out there?"

So there were more nymphs or guards. Great. I glanced at the castle to see both men and woman nymphs running outside, carrying swords and tridents.

This was not going to be fun.

I kept running. Luckily I was closer to the scythe than any of them were, but they were gaining on me fast. I reached out and took the scythe by the snath.

That was when everything changed.

I should have known there would be some sort of strange energy with it, but I wasn't prepared for it. It was as if energy of the primordial era rushed into me. It felt as if it were going to tear me apart. I screamed as the blast almost blew me away. Then, as quick as it came, it subsided and I understood—I understood what this scythe was and why it came into existence. It was meant to destroy—it was created in fear, and it was meant to destroy.

Taking a deep breath, I tried to calm myself down. This wasn't my first rodeo when it came to having a dark energy inside that wanted to destroy everything. No, I was used to it. It was my nature. This thing couldn't distract me from what I needed to do.

The nymphs attacked me from behind, and I was quick to use the snath of the scythe to block their attacks. I wasn't going to use it against them, as I didn't think they deserved it, not to mention it would be overkill. I felt that if I swung this thing, I would destroy this entire place, and although Amphitrite was kind of a bitch and Poseidon was here and I could kill him all over again, I wasn't that cruel.

Although, I had to admit, I kind of wanted to.

But these nymphs didn't deserve that. They were just following orders. I smacked them with the blunt end, blowing them all back and making a run for it toward the entrance and where Peisy and Mel were battling their own people. Peisy used her voice to knock them all back, and as I approached, she grabbed both our hands, and we went through the bubble into the sea.

So apparently, once I went somewhere with air, the whole breathing underwater thing wasn't a thing. Also, the current was strong the moment you went from inside the bubble to the water, and we were all pulled up and away.

I opened my mouth, and it filled with water. I was choking as Peisy turned and kissed me on the lips. I took in deep breaths of whatever I was breathing, happy that I was no longer drowning. She went over and did the same to Mel, who appeared as relieved as I was. We began swimming away as quickly as we could.

As I was about to snap my fingers and make the rope, I felt something stab me in the back. I screamed out in pain as I let go of Peisy's hand.

"Chrys!" she screamed as I turned around and found that it was Poseidon who had stabbed me with his trident.

How stupid was he? I watched as red filled the water around me. Everything seemed a bit fuzzy as more and more blood came out of me.

He raised his trident as if he were going to do it again. I blocked it with the snath.

"Why won't you just die?" Poseidon yelled.

"Why won't you just stop being an asshole!" I yelled back.

Peisy and Mel swam toward us, but I shook my head. "Stay back! I'll handle this."

I pushed the snath toward him, sending him backward, and with one quick motion, I sliced through the water with the scythe.

And damn, it really was powerful. I never would have expected that it was so easy to wield.

The blade cut the water in half, which I didn't think was possible, destroyed Poseidon in a second, but the powerful wave didn't stop there. No, it went straight back and straight for the palace.

"Oh no," I whispered as I watched the entire palace

explode.

I never meant to hurt them—I was just trying to stop Poseidon.

The impact sent the three of us flying backward. I didn't know which way was up or down as currents grabbed me and hauled me off. Blood mixed with the water around me as I kept bleeding out. It was too much for me, and as I clutched the scythe, I lost sight of Peisy and Mel and eventually lost consciousness.

CHAPTER 16

Huntley

Where was Chrys?

I had gone back to my room to change, as I didn't have any cool, snappy powers to change like Pothos did. He offered to change my shirt for me, but that always felt weird to me. Also, I didn't trust that he would pick a shirt I liked. And I wanted to walk around a bit.

As I tried to clear my head, I worried about Chrys. They had gotten up to earth before we did, and we had to travel all the way back. Why wasn't she back yet? Pothos had mentioned gods couldn't snap to places in the water due to the currents and something about

Poseidon. I supposed it was the same in Olympus and the underworld, so it made sense. But still, I didn't like having to wait.

I also didn't like being around all these gods without her. I felt that I didn't belong, and at least with her, I could hide behind her. I tried doing that with Hades, and he simply gave me a look. No, it was too awkward. There was always Persephone, as she liked me, but again, awkward.

At least I had Pothos, but I felt bad hiding behind him when he was dealing with his own problems. His brother had been eaten by Kronos. I supposed it was better than being dead, as he could still be saved, but still. I had no idea what kind of agony he was going through currently. I wondered if it was like all the stories of whales eating people or if it was like they were in darkness, like a pit. If it was anything like Tartarus, it would more than likely be the latter. Either way, it wouldn't be fun and we needed to do something about it.

I got to Chrys's and my bedroom and grabbed a new black tee and threw the other one in the sink to deal with later. I sighed as I peered over at Chrys's setup. She would be okay—she had to be. It was normal to take longer. Not much time had passed either way. She would be fine. I took a deep breath and headed back to where all the gods were.

As I made my way through the hallway, I found Hades pinching the bridge of his nose. That was his typical stressed-out look. I wondered what part of all this madness he was stressed out about the most. Chrys still not returning, Kronos destroying everything, Aether taking over Olympus, Tartarus not having a lock, or if it was because all these gods were in their domain, causing problems. I had a feeling it was a little bit of everything.

I tried to sneak past, as it didn't appear he wanted to be bothered, when he opened his eyes.

"Oh, Huntley, it's you." He let out a sigh. "I was worried it was one of them. Or worse, Zeus."

"Just me. I had to change my shirt because of Ares's blood and all that."

"I'm surprise it wasn't your blood. He doesn't usually just threaten but likes to get in a few punches."

I shrugged. "Yeah, but Aphrodite was there, so he wasn't able to. And he's a bit weak with the whole Hephaestus beating him into a pulp and all."

He shook his head. "I knew it was a bad idea for him

to go, but he never listens. He cares about Aphrodite and wants her to be safe even if it's at the cost of his life. One of the few godly couples that actually love each other."

He had a point there—I didn't know of any other gods that truly loved each other. There were flings and marriages, but did I know of any that were still together? None came to mind, but at the same time, I wasn't well acquainted with many.

"But I suppose I should get back in there. I am this domain's ruler after all." He began to walk when suddenly he clutched his chest and bent over.

I stepped forward. "Are you all right?"

He didn't move as he grimaced. Whatever was happening appeared to hurt bad. "I was afraid this would happen."

"What?" I asked.

He took a few deep breaths and stood straight up. "These bodies—they weren't meant to be outside the afterlife for long."

I didn't like the sound of that. "What are you saying?"

"I'm saying that once Tartarus has a lock and Kronos is back where he belongs, all the souls that were in there will also go back. Including myself."

So all this had been for nothing? I couldn't believe that. Hades had to be freed of Tartarus or else I didn't think Chrys was going to be able to handle it. What would she do when she found out? I had a feeling it wouldn't be good.

"Huntley, you have to promise me you won't tell Chrys. We have to finish this, and I can't distract her with this. Will you promise me?"

I didn't like the idea of lying to Chrys, but he had a point. "I promise. But there has to be a way to free you…"

"There isn't. At least not that I know of. I already feel weak—I don't know how much longer I'll be able to go on like this. Chrys needs to get back here soon. How long did Hephaestus say it would take him?"

"The day after tomorrow the lock will be ready," I said.

He nodded. "Good. Zeus and I should be able to last that long. We can at least help from the sidelines."

"Is that why the two of you didn't come with us?"

"Yeah, I assume Zeus noticed as well. He didn't want to risk it by going with you. Also because Hephaestus hates him as much as he hates Ares."

"Is there anyone who doesn't hate Zeus?" I asked.

Hades chuckled. "I suppose not. Maybe those random human women who are seduced by him. But other than that, I think everyone has some kind of beef with him."

Especially Hades since Zeus tried to take his daughter away.

He patted my back. "But let's get back to the others. I'm sure Persephone wants to be relieved soon."

"I don't blame her."

We walked down the hallway. It was strange being around him again after everything that had happened. I didn't want to think that after all this was over, he would be sent back to Tartarus. It wasn't fair. I would trade anything for him to be free.

We stopped in front of the door, and Hades put his hand on my shoulder.

"Huntley, there is one more thing."

I turned to him, afraid it was one more disaster. "What is it?"

"Thank you for taking care of my daughter. And keeping this place running. I'm sure it hasn't been easy. I can rest easy now knowing that this place is fine without me."

I didn't know what to say—it wasn't like him to compliment me like that. I shook my head. "No, it's not fine. It needs you. Chrys needs you. It hasn't been easy."

"Don't worry about me. Just live on, all right. Promise me you both will forget about me and keep pushing forward. The gate cannot be opened again—the world cannot face this kind of destruction again. Do you hear me?"

I slowly nodded. "Yeah. I'll try."

That was a complete and utter lie. There was no way that Chrys would forget her father. He was everything to her. I knew her, and I knew she would try again. I would have to tell her when she got back—I would have to help her figure out how to stop all this.

We stepped into the lounge area, and all the gods and nymphs were huddled together, drinking tea and eating pastries. Zeus was lying on the lounge chair, being fed grapes like a classic Roman movie.

Hades went over and smacked him in the back of the head. I held back a laugh.

Zeus grabbed his head. "What was that for?"

Hades glared at him. "Your people are here, suffering, and you are being fed grapes. Help my wife calm everyone down."

"They're used to me being king—I was reminding them of the good times."

"The good times?" Hades clutched his fists. "Since you've been king of Olympus, there have been no good times!"

Gods started to gather around, as they clearly all liked drama. Pothos made his way over to me with a smile.

"I have to admit, all the drama with the underworld has been high quality," Pothos commented. His brother Anteros stepped up with him, nodding.

"Yeah… It gets old," I said as we watched the fight continue.

Zeus stood up. "You know what Hades? You are a—"

Suddenly out of nowhere a figure fell from the ceiling and landed on the lounge chair with a loud thud, causing it to break. The whole room was silent as we all stared at the strange figure.

Zeus was the first to say anything. "Poseidon?"

CHAPTER 17

Chrys

All I saw was darkness. But that could have been the fact that my eyes were still shut.

I opened them as I took a deep breath, which had been a big mistake. Now my mouth was full of sand. I coughed and tried to spit out as much as I could, but it was no use—the sand was stuck to my tongue and inside my cheeks. I could feel it even in my teeth.

As I looked around, I found I was surrounded by sand. A wave came up behind me, pushing me up onto the beach a bit. I stood up and felt pain shoot through my body. I peered down to find blood everywhere.

That was right. Poseidon had stabbed me. That

bastard.

Well, he was definitely dead, as was everyone in that palace. I felt bad about that, but it was his fault. He should have let me go. But no, he had to keep being an asshole that was in my way. But now we knew where he went—straight to his wife so he could get some action. I shook my head. He had left his brothers in the underworld so that they could deal with the problem.

Father and Zeus were not going to be happy when they heard about that. But nonetheless, he was probably with them now. Or in Tartarus. To be honest, I had no idea what would have happened to him since Tartarus wasn't closed and no souls were going there. Did he go to Elysium? He didn't deserve it if he did. No, he was probably somewhere else. All the other souls that got hit by that blast were probably in Elysium though. I would have to go out there and apologize later, but they were in paradise and there really wasn't more one could ask for.

First I would need to deal with the problem at hand— all this blood and the fact I was dizzy. Nothing made sense, and I tried to remember what I had gone into the ocean for. Right, it was for the scythe. I peered around and saw it lying on the sand a few feet away. That was lucky. I must have had a death grip on it. Then I remembered Peisy and Mel. I glanced around but didn't see any sign of them.

"Crap," I whispered. "Where was I?"

In the distance there was a small cottage. It was blurry, as was everything else. I squinted and tried to make it out. It appeared familiar.

"Circe?" I said as I collapsed to my knees and passed out again.

When I opened my eyes again, I found I was no longer on the beach but lying in a bed. I stared up at a familiar wooden ceiling. My heart began to beat really fast as I bolted up. No, I couldn't be back in this place—last time I was here I had been drugged.

Pain shot through my body. I grimaced.

"Don't worry, you are safe here. Prometheus and Apollo aren't around."

I turned to find Circe was standing at the dresser, mixing some herbs. Her graying hair was pulled back in a loose ponytail, and she wore her typical loose and flowy dress. She grabbed a cloth and placed the wet mixture on it.

"I have no idea how you found this place—nor do I

want to know. It took me forever to move to a new island."

I glanced around. "This is a new island? It looks exactly the same."

"It's the same building. I moved it over, but the island is different. I suppose you didn't get a good look since you were bleeding out and all that. You are lucky I was just coming back from harvesting some plants."

"Thank you for saving me. But I am in a hurry and need to get out of here." I moved the sheets over and grimaced. Damn that trident hurt.

"What? Do you need to go use that scythe to kill Kronos or something?"

The scythe was leaning against the wall next to the door. I nodded. "Yeah, something like that."

She brought over the compress. "I'm not going to stop you, as I don't want to see this world destroyed, but let me heal your wounds first. This won't take long, not with my magic and your strength."

I turned my back to her so she could place the compress on my wound. The coolness made it sting for a second, and then it quickly stopped and began to feel better.

"By the look of it, I would guess Poseidon did this to

you."

I nodded. "Yep. He escaped Tartarus with Kronos. Zeus and my father are in the underworld still. They had no idea he escaped so quickly."

"That's definitely something he would do."

The more we talked, the better I felt. The herbs she used worked fast. "Did anyone else wash up on the shore? I was in the water with two friends—Mel and Peisy."

She shook her head. "No, you were the only one. My guess is that they traveled farther in hopes you would make it. The sea is a large place—it wouldn't be wise for them to keep looking for you unless you didn't show up for a while."

I nodded. That made sense. "I thank you very much for helping me and healing me. But I must go. My father is waiting for me, and I don't want him to worry."

"You do know that your father and the rest of them will go back to Tartarus once you defeat Kronos, right?"

I frowned. "Amphitrite mentioned something about that. I can't let my father go to Tartarus—I'll do anything."

"I am sure you'll find a way to sever the ties they have with the underworld—but I'll warn you, it won't be easy. There're many things stronger than the bond of death."

I sighed. "Yeah. I know."

She went over to her mixture of herbs and grabbed more of the fresh plants she had. "Take these with you. I have a feeling that there will be many warriors who will need them in the coming months. I'm sure Maka will be able to figure out my formula and make good use of it all."

"Oh, you know Maka?"

She nodded. "Yes, I do. We were friends a long time ago, but that was in the past."

"Why don't you come with me? We could really use your help."

She shook her head. "No, none of the gods care for me anymore. Besides, if Kronos does find me here, I have lived a long time and feel that this would be spot to end it all. I have accepted death. I have been alive for a while and am ready to rest. Young gods like yourself need to take over, just like we took over after the titans."

I understood what she meant but wasn't too happy

that she didn't want to help. I stood up, my body feeling better now that the herbs had done their thing. Circe handed me the herbs.

"Thank you for everything. You saved me."

"It was my pleasure to pay you back for what happened with Prometheus. I didn't want to drug you like I did, and I am sorry."

"Don't worry, all was forgiven. I understood why Prometheus did what he did."

She gave me a hug, and I went to grab my scythe, and in a moment, I disappeared and reappeared in front of the gates of the underworld.

And I couldn't believe what I saw.

Kronos was destroying everything. Fires burned throughout the world and tears filled my eyes.

I had to make sure the lock was on Tartarus before I could take him out. I clutched my scythe, wanting to end him right then and there, but I couldn't. I took a deep breath and turned to the doors of the underworld.

Just like Circe predicted, Mel and Peisy were there. They hugged me quickly.

"Thank goodness you are all right!" Mel exclaimed.

"We were worried. I would have gone looking for you if you were any later."

"Thank you. Both of you. I was saved by Circe, and all is fine now. Let's get going so we can end this once and for all."

CHAPTER 18

Huntley

Chrys was back.

I ran to the dock to find Chrys getting off one of the gondolas. I swept her off her feet in a hug.

"Careful! I am still healing." She laughed.

I set her down, and she gave me a kiss. Now that I looked at her, she did appear to have stab wounds in her back.

"What happened? Are you okay?"

She nodded. "I'm fine. It was just an incident, but Circe healed me up and sent me home with some herbs." She held up a basket. "They should help anyone who is injured."

"That's good," I said. "Ares got beat up pretty badly and will need some."

"Ares? Wasn't he with you? Are you all right?"

"I'm fine. Hephaestus and Ares just have some anger issues."

"Ah. Right. Well, which way are they?" she asked as she grabbed another object out of the gondola. It was the scythe.

The scythe was beautiful—a jade-like color that shone brightly in the light. I had never seen a weapon so beautiful and yet so deadly.

"In the secondary lounge? I didn't even know we had one. I swore that room was just a closet."

"Father can make rooms appear and disappear. I can too but haven't needed to."

"Ah," I said. "That would make sense."

"Did your mission go well?" Mel asked as she got out of the gondola. Peisy followed after her.

I nodded. "Yeah, I think Hades wanted to go over everything together. But it should be good."

"I'm glad." Chrys gave me a kiss on my cheek. "That means this is all almost over."

There was a sadness in her voice. I wondered if she knew the truth about her father and how he would have to go back into Tartarus. I would bring it up later, though, as she didn't need more stress at the moment.

We all headed toward the second lounge when Poseidon stepped out into the hallway. Chrys quickly pulled up her scythe as if she were going to attack him.

I grabbed her arm. "What are you doing?"

"He was the one who tried to kill me! Again!"

"Well," Poseidon beamed. "You deserved it."

Hades and Zeus stepped out into the hallway. Hades glanced at his daughter. "What is going on here?"

"This bastard tried to kill me in the ocean!" She tried to swing the scythe down, but Hades caught it by the snath.

"Do not swing that in here! You'll destroy everything."

She frowned. "He deserves it."

"You may fight him and beat him into a pulp, but first give me the scythe."

Chrys handed the scythe over to him and then set the herbs down. She tossed her hair back and then punched Poseidon straight in the jaw. He went down with a loud thud.

"Yeah! Get him!" Mel yelled. Peisy was right next to her, cheering her on. They both clearly wanted to see the bastard pay. I could imagine Peisy did as Poseidon had killed her sisters.

She jumped on top of him, punching him and pulling at his hair. I was surprised Zeus was just standing there, watching his brother get beaten. I thought they were closer knit than that. I guess I was wrong.

I was also surprised that Poseidon didn't seem to be able to fight back, or he was holding back. I had a feeling it was the former as he seemed weak. I wasn't sure if that was because she had just killed him with the scythe and sent him down here, or if it was how Hades felt weak, as he shouldn't have been away from Tartarus.

It was a good five minutes before Hades pulled his daughter off Poseidon. "That's enough. I think he gets the message."

"I disagree," Chrys commented as she straightened her clothes. "But we have more important matters to discuss."

Zeus watched as his brother tried to stand up. Poseidon eyed him. "You know, you could have helped me."

Zeus shrugged. "It was fun to watch a girl kick your ass."

Poseidon sighed as he stood up. I snuck past him after Chrys as she headed to her father's study. I watched the scythe shimmer in the low lighting the castle always consisted of. So that was what adamantine looked like. I had expected it to be more like the silver-colored metal in *X-Men*, but I supposed that was fiction.

Once we got to the study, Hades gestured for us all to sit. There weren't many chairs, so I pulled one out for Chrys to sit in and then stood behind her, leaning on the back of the chair. Zeus sat down, tilting back like he owned the place while Poseidon stayed near the door, leaning against the wall.

Hades set the scythe down on the desk. Chrys kept her eyes on it but didn't say anything.

"All right, start from the beginning," Hades said.

Chrys sighed. "Well, we traveled to Amphitrite's palace. It was a long swim and not something I ever want to do again. We get there and talk to her. She refuses to give me the scythe and then Poseidon appears, in the nude. Seems they just wanted to be together and…" She trailed off. "She gave us the shield but didn't give us the scythe. As I walked out, I heard it calling to me and found it."

"You could hear it?" Hades asked as he glanced at his brothers.

She nodded. "Yes, but it speaks in primordial, so I don't understand it."

Zeus laughed. "Well, that's a fun twist. She can hear the deity that's in the scythe."

"What?" Chrys asked. "What deity is in it?"

"Uranus," Hades answered. "The original primordial god that this was used to slay."

The room was quiet for a moment. I had no idea what that all meant, so I just kept my mouth shut.

Poseidon broke the silence. "Where she found it was also not where we put the scythe. It was kept in a special room but appeared outside in with all the junk Amphitrite has. I have no idea how it did that."

"So it chose Chrys and she gets to wield it this time." Zeus leaned back more and put his hands behind his head. "Well, it's almost as if that prophecy came true."

Hades glared at him. "All of which you started. If you had just left her alone, none of this would have happened. You do realize all the prophecies just make you paranoid and you do stupid things that cause the prophecies to come true right? Like Kronos for example. He was told that we all would be his end, and so he tried to kill us all, which made us kill him."

That was a really good point. I wondered how many prophecies this applied to.

"Whatever brother, you know I am right."

Hades pinched the bridge of his nose. "Go on, daughter."

"Then we made a run for it, and Poseidon stabbed me with his trident. Then I swung the scythe because he pissed me off, and it was a bit more powerful than I expected. I think there might be a gaping hole where the palace once stood." She whispered that last part.

"That's right, she destroyed my love and my home. She should be punished," Poseidon commented.

Hades didn't even answer him. "Continue."

"I passed out from the loss of blood and woke to find Circe helping me. She healed up my wounds and gave me some herbs to give to Maka. Then I came here."

Hades glanced up at me. "Huntley, summarize your experience for her so she can be caught up as well."

I nodded. "Right. We went to Hephaestus's volcano. Ares got the living daylights beat out of him. Aphrodite stopped Hephaestus from killing Ares, and Hephaestus finally agreed to make the lock. He said it would be ready the day after tomorrow, but that was a few hours ago, so more like less than that now."

"Sounds like you had quite the adventure too." Chrys smiled.

"So," Hades began, "between now and when Huntley will go and get the lock, you'll need to train. Then when Huntley goes to retrieve the lock, you can battle Kronos."

I held up my hand. "Shouldn't she wait until I get back? Otherwise we would be cutting it close, right?"

Hades shook his head. "We don't have a moment to waste. With every passing second, Kronos is destroying more and more, and Aether may have taken over Olympus already. The battles are getting intense. I trust you'll retrieve it quickly and be back here in no time. I'll have Hermes go with you as well. Once he gets back."

I slowly nodded. "Right. I guess when you put it that way. I'll be as quick as I can."

CHAPTER 19

Chrys

After a good night's sleep, I began my day training with Thanatos. He was rather good at handling a scythe and in teaching me how to fight with it. We, of course, practice with regular scythes and not the scythe I would be fighting with, as that might destroy the castle and the underworld.

We were training in the gym again after taking a long lunch and making sure everyone who came to the underworld today were taken care of. There were still a lot of gods coming down here, but I didn't see any that would have been from Olympus lately. We had no word other than we were waiting for Hermes to report back what Aether was up to.

If gods died in that battle against Aether, they would have been sent to Elysium Fields. Although Father kept track of everyone who died, with everything currently going on, it was piling up and he hadn't taken a chance to look to see if gods such as Hera and Artemis were killed. Even if they hadn't been killed, there was also the possibility that Aether kidnapped them all and took over Olympus. That's why we were waiting. If nothing bad had happened, he should be back soon.

Thanatos swung his scythe at me, and I blocked it with the snath. The blades were made of wood, but it would still hurt if I got hit by it. I twirled my scythe around and swept under his legs, causing him to fall to the ground.

"Very good," Thanatos said as I helped him up. "I think you are a natural for this."

"I'm not sure if that's a compliment or not." I went over to the bench and grabbed a towel to wipe off some sweat.

"What, is there something wrong with using a scythe as a weapon?" Thanatos asked as grabbed some water.

I shook my head. "No, that's not the problem—the problem is more that the scythe picked me to wield it.

Father and Zeus were acting like that was a bad thing—as if I was the only dark person who could deal with its presence."

He took a seat and patted the bench next to him. I took a seat.

"The scythe of Kronos was created by Gaia to defeat Uranus. Its purpose was always death. It is hard for anyone who doesn't deal with death to wield it because that dark energy—the energy of revenge and death—still possesses it. And when Uranus was destroyed by it, his energy went into it. Then Zeus, to free his brothers and sisters, used it to defeat Kronos. Not even Zeus could stand being around the scythe and threw it in the ocean."

I took in the story. So Zeus didn't like being around it either but wasn't sure why he thought throwing it in the ocean would work. Someone was bound to find it.

"It can corrupt the strongest of minds, but you seem to be fine. You understand life and death, so you aren't at as great a risk. You are stronger than you know, Chrys."

"So that's why my father sent me after it—he knew?"

He nodded. "Yes. He was able to wield it for some time and probably could have kept it, but you know

Zeus and his jealousy—he didn't want his brother to be stronger than him."

I rolled my eyes. That sounded about right. "I just don't know how I feel about it. I mean, I can hear his voice, but I couldn't understand it."

"That's probably a good thing. If you could understand it, it might make you even more susceptible to whatever it's saying."

I shrugged. "Maybe. I like to think I am a bit stronger than that."

Thanatos ruffled the top of my head. "You are still young. Don't worry about it too much. Just defeat Kronos and Aether first."

Before I could answer him, the door to the gym opened. It was Huntley.

"Hermes is back, and Hades is filling him in. I figured you wanted to hear what is going on in Olympus as well."

I got up. Of course I did. I hurried after him and headed into the study where my father was talking to Hermes.

Overall, Hermes didn't seem to be injured, but it appeared as if he were covered in other people's blood and ash. He glanced at me, his hair disheveled and seeming like he had seen the most horrible things.

I sat down next to him and grabbed his hand. "What happened?"

"Aether has taken over Olympus. I was able to get Hera out but not without her getting severely wounded. Artemis and Athena are now on his side. He… Even if you defeat Kronos, I don't know if we'll be able to take him out. He's the god of the aether—he is more powerful than we could have even imagined."

I frowned. Great. Once one strong titan was destroyed, I would need to battle a primordial god. "The scythe should defeat him—it defeated Uranus."

"We can only hope. But he's gathering up his children and now rules over any god whose home is in Olympus. You'll be alone and may have to fight against some of our own."

I shrugged. "It's not like that would be a first. There were always gods against me. I think I can do it."

"If all gods of Olympus have to serve him, then what are you doing here, Hermes?" Hades asked. "Are you not a god of Olympus?"

He shook his head. "No. I technically serve Zeus and Zeus alone. But I'm also just sort of someone who does my own thing…"

Hades rolled his eyes but didn't say anything.

"I can defeat him. I know I can," I said as I stood up. "I'll defeat Kronos and then I'll send Aether to Tartarus where he belongs."

Hermes nodded. "I trust you'll try your hardest, but I fear this is the end of Olympus as we know it."

"Hermes," Hades began. "I need you to take Huntley to Hephaestus. You are the fastest to get there and back, and we need the lock as soon as possible. Can you do that for me?"

He nodded. "I can."

"Then in the morning, you'll take Chrys and Huntley to where they need to be. And then we'll end this battle once and for all."

The rest of the day went by and morning came. Huntley and I stood together, waiting for Hermes to take us where we needed to go. I held the scythe tight in my hand, ready to battle Kronos. I even had some healing herbs from Circe if need be. This had been all my fault —only I would be able to take him down.

It was apparent my father didn't want to leave the underworld. I wasn't sure if it was because he felt he needed to make sure everything was fine in my absence or if it had to do with his soul being dead. Zeus also didn't offer to come with, but that could have been out of laziness or pride. Either way, I didn't want him to come along anyway.

My father and mother embraced me, hugging me tight, knowing I might not come back from this. I should have been more scared, but this wasn't the first time I had almost lost my life, and I had a feeling it wouldn't be the last. I needed to do this, or the whole world would be destroyed.

I held the scythe and shield, ready to go into battle. I felt like a warrior even though I knew I wasn't one. I was just a girl trying to survive.

I smiled at my parents. "I'll be fine. Don't worry. I am your daughter after all."

My mother held back tears. "You better come straight back here. We'll gather reinforcements to attack Aether. Please don't forget that."

I nodded. "I'll come back here. I promise."

Persephone hugged me once more, and my father kissed my head. "You'll do fine. I know you will."

"Thank you."

I turned to Hermes and grabbed on to him as did Huntley. Hermes took us up in the air, but like last time, he didn't make me cover my eyes. I found the one spot in Oceanus that it was possible to fly through. Hermes knew it would be a hassle to try to cover our eyes, and he probably felt that the world was going to end as well. Who cared if we knew where this entrance was.

We made it to earth, and I still couldn't believe my eyes. Everything was dusted in ash. Human bodies covered the ground, dead from either the fire, hunger, or disease. It smelled foul, and I wanted to throw up. But I had to focus—I had to go find Kronos.

Huntley did throw up. I couldn't blame him, as he too was human. I didn't like seeing these bodies, and I had a feeling it was even more upsetting to him. I was used to death but not in this form.

"Hermes, take Huntley out of here quickly. This is no place for a human."

He nodded and went to grab Huntley.

Huntley shook his head. "No, not without your promising me you'll be all right."

I turned to him and wrapped my arms around him. "I'll be all right. Promise me you'll be fine."

"I promise."

We kissed, and I knew in my heart it wouldn't be the last time I saw him. Everything would be all right.

Hermes grabbed Huntley, and they both disappeared. I turned to the field of death and called out, "Kronos, I am here to fight!"

CHAPTER 20

Huntley

A moment later, we were back on the volcano in front of the lake. The sky, as it was everywhere in the world, was dark. I threw up some more, both from the transportation and from seeing all those bodies. No one deserved to be killed in such a manner. It was morbid and vile. I just prayed that their souls were able to make it into the underworld.

"Are you all right?" Hermes asked.

I slowly nodded. "Yeah, or at least I will be. It's just so wrong."

"Yeah. I know. I've been traveling around for some time now, checking the world out. Most of the places appeared like that. There are some areas that he hasn't gotten to, but for the most part… I don't know what's going to happen to this place once he's defeated. Though it wouldn't be the first time earth was almost destroyed, and it won't be the last."

"Life finds a way?" I asked with a slight smirk.

"That it does."

I wasn't sure he got my reference but stood up. "The entrance is over there on that side of the lake. Do you think you can transport us over?"

He shook his head. "I don't want to make you barf. I'll just fly us over—that will be easier."

"Right."

He picked me up and began to fly over the lake. Even though the sky was dark, the lake still had a strong blue tint. It was rather beautiful, and I wished I could swim in it. Then again, I was already dead and it should have been fine. Maybe. I might get stuck in some random spot in the underworld, like a game that put you in a random spot. I didn't want to find out the hard way.

We were almost halfway across the water when I heard laughter come from above us. Hermes and I both glanced up to find three figures floating in the sky.

"Ah shit," Hermes mumbled.

"Well, well, well, what do we have here?" the figure on the left asked as he flew down to be closer to us. Hermes stopped in his tracks, and I felt like a sitting duck.

"Move aside, Ania. This doesn't concern you."

"Actually, it does! We three can't let you pass because, well, you know what will happen once the lock is back on Tartarus, don't you? All the souls will slowly be sucked back in."

Ania was closer to me now and appeared, well, sort of like a circus performer. As the other two flew closer, I noticed they were dressed the same. Why couldn't we ever face normal gods?

"Well, that doesn't seem to be my fault," Hermes said. "And the world is sort of being destroyed, so move out of the way or I'll force you to."

Ania laughed again, his red curls tossing back as he did so. The green of his vest and headband stood out even though it was dark. The other two wore similar vests, headbands, and white pants, but they were different colors—one had a blue vest and headband and the other a purple. They all had curly red hair, however, and it would have been hard to tell them apart if it weren't for the vests.

"Hermes, the only reason we daimons were put in Tartarus is because you gods couldn't handle us. Now, do you really think you can handle three on your own with a human to try to keep safe?"

They had a point—because Hermes was carrying me, we both were sitting ducks. Hermes knew this, so he flew back and toward the side of the lake.

"Ah, ah, not so fast!" one of the two others called after.

Hermes made a grunting sound and dropped me. I screamed as I fell to the water, which wouldn't kill me but would probably suck, when I felt something grab my wrist. Hermes threw me over to the trail, and I landed on the stones, scratching my skin up and bruising my left knee.

"Owww." I whimpered as Hermes collapsed beside me. I glanced over at him to find that his wings were bleeding. "Damn, you okay?"

He coughed as he stood. "No. I'm not. These three are assholes."

"Who are they anyway?" I asked as I glanced up at the triplets.

"They're Ania, Achos, and Lupa, who are the daimons of pain, grief, and distress."

"Let me guess. They're Aether's sons."

"Bingo."

I cracked my knuckles. "Well then, let's get this started."

Achos came at me, and I punched him straight in his chilled-jawed face. He went flying back into the lake. I was surprised I could hit him with such force, but I had been training for a couple of years now.

I grinned, but it was short-lived as Lupa swooped down and grabbed me by the back of the shirt, carrying me straight up. I yelled as I tried to get him to let go. I saw Hermes fly up to catch me, but he grimaced. Whatever they did to his wings, it looked like they hurt.

"And up and up we go!"

I kept flailing to get him to let me go. As I reached both hands up, the stupidest thing happened—I fell out of my shirt.

Now I was shirtless and falling toward a bunch of rocks. This was going to hurt. Hermes ran toward me and was able to catch me. We both tumbled to the ground.

"Sorry about that," I said as I got off him.

"You owe me."

I nodded in agreement as we both got up and stood

back-to-back. Hermes had put his wings away, but I could see blood on his shirt that hadn't been there before.

The three daimons laughed as they circled us. They pulled out their knives and made swipes as they flew in.

"We don't happen to have weapons, do we?" I asked.

"Honestly, Huntley, I didn't think we would get attacked in this short of distance to Hephaestus. Also," he turned and yelled at the mountain, "if he would just come out with all his own weapons, this would be over quickly!"

There was no answer. I half thought maybe Hephaestus would step outside and save us, but he was a no-show. I turned back to the maniacal trio as they sliced and stabbed. I really wished I wasn't shirtless at the moment, as that was making this all the worse.

As Achos came straight at me, his purple headband clinging to his head as I had punched him into the water, I watched his hand carefully and grabbed his wrist, pulling him along so he couldn't stab me. I caught him off guard, and he loosened his grip on the knife. I was able to take it out of his hand and kick him back in the water. He screamed in a high-pitched squeal as he saw the water coming straight at him.

"I got us a knife!" I said, holding it up to Hermes.

"Good job. Now make sure not to lose it."

I nodded and turned to the next daimon that was attacking. He pointed the knife down at me, and I blocked it with my own. Hermes, however, didn't have as much luck as Ania stabbed him straight in the back. He let out a scream.

"Hermes!" I exclaimed as I hurried to him, fighting off Ania as he laughed and stabbed Hermes again. I was able to stab Ania in the leg. He let out a hiss and swung his knife at me, knocking mine out of my hand.

"Shit!" I yelled as I fell back. Ania held the knife straight under my chin.

"Ready to die, human?" Ania's lips curled. "Or should I torture you for funsies?"

"I'm already dead," I said even though I knew this wasn't the time or place. "I'm actually the prince of the underworld and whatnot."

Ania narrowed his eyes. "You? Prince of the underworld?" He laughed. "No wonder Tartarus was unlocked with someone like you in charge."

"Hey, that's not—" Actually, that was fair. I wasn't fit to be a ruler.

"Well, it's no matter. I'm going to cut you into little

bits anyway!" He raised his knife up, and I shut my eyes.

But there was nothing. I kept listening when suddenly I heard a thud. I opened my eyes to find Ania's head rolling on the ground next to his body. Looking up, I found Prometheus standing above his body.

"Miss me?" he asked with a smirk.

CHAPTER 21

Chrys

Okay, the fear was starting to kick in. My arms shook as I watched the giant dark figure make his way over to me. I had never seen anything so horrific in my life. He appeared like a ghost, and as he walked across the land, destruction was in its wake. It was almost as if he were death.

But he wasn't death. Death was not as destructive as this.

Death was kind, as Thanatos was considered to be the god of death. He cared for souls. It was apparent that Kronos did not. He appeared to want to eradicate it all, as he gave no respect to any of it. I clutched my scythe even tighter. I wouldn't let him get away with this. I couldn't.

As the creature came toward me, he slowly shrank. I thought at first it was my eyes playing tricks on me, but I soon realized that wasn't the case. He was almost my size when his dark, shadowlike figure was now that of a normal human-appearing god.

He was older-looking, which wasn't a surprise, but I had been so used to all the gods appearing like they were in their prime. He, on the other hand, appeared like he was in his late fifties or sixties in the human world.

Kronos brought his hands behind his back. "Well, if it isn't the daughter of Hades—the girl who freed me. I should be thanking you, you know. I was able to leave that nasty place because of you."

I twirled the scythe in my hand. "And I am here to send you back."

He let out a deep chuckle. "Oh yeah? I can tell there is no lock on Tartarus yet. Where exactly are you going to send me?"

I frowned. I couldn't tell him what our plan was, or he might go after Huntley.

"Or do you think you can destroy me completely?"

He raised his arm and gestured around. "You know, I was one of the first gods in existence that helped make this world the way it is. I was worshipped as the titan of harvest, but then my children destroyed me."

"Because you tried to kill them first," I said. "They only wanted to escape your wrath."

"And is that what you are doing? Escaping my wrath?"

"Not escaping—stopping. You are destroying the entire world. If you wanted to be free, why didn't you just hide? Instead, you made yourself known by killing."

"I wanted to hide—wanted to survive a little longer, but once I saw what the humans were up to—how they have been demolishing this planet, I had to stop it all. Then once I have a clear slate, I can repair it all and start over, without humans. They were a mistake—Prometheus created them, so they had little chance of being of any help."

I shook my head. "No, there are plenty of humans that are good! It is the gods' fault that there are so many problems. They turned their backs on them."

He let out another laugh. "Oh, you naive little girl. Let me guess. You fell in love with a human? Well, I have news for you—they all disappoint. After a few decades, maybe centuries, your human will get sick of you. They don't understand eternity, even in the underworld. That's why the river of Lethe exists—so they forget themselves and live in peace."

I knew that was why the river was there, but I knew Huntley wasn't like that. We would be together forever, and neither of us would be sick of each other.

"Even your father and brother got sick of each other, and they were gods. Those who don't belong in the underworld will always hate it."

"No! My father and mother love each other! It is because of the gods that they fell out of love."

He raised an eyebrow. "Is it? Or is it because they had to hide their precious daughter?"

"That isn't what happened!" I yelled. "It was because of the other gods always causing problems and bad-mouthing my father."

He gestured to the world. "Then you agree they deserve all this."

"No— I… It doesn't matter, the humans don't deserve this."

"You don't think so? Do you realize how many humans go to Tartarus on a daily basis? I do. You judge many that are in a moral gray area—you know how dark many of them are. They don't deserve this place."

I had to admit, there were a lot of humans who didn't deserve anything better than death and an eternity in Tartarus. There were countless souls down there, but that didn't mean they all deserved to be destroyed. There were still a lot who went to Asphodel Fields. There were people who grew up in conditions that maybe they were morally gray, but given the chance, would do good. I was fighting for them—I was fighting for the gods who had my back, and not to mention, it was my fault Kronos had been unleashed.

Raising my scythe, I shook my head. "You will not turn me with your lies. I'll end you once and for all."

He chuckled. "Suit yourself. But for the record, after watching what has been going on in the world over all these years, I have to say, you are my favorite offspring."

I didn't know how to take that and said nothing as his figure grew and turned into shadowy darkness once again. I swung the scythe at him, but he moved and the powerful slice split the ground in two. I gasped at how much destruction it caused even though I had seen what it did to Poseidon and his palace.

But at least this area of the world had already been decimated. I didn't have to worry as much.

Kronos's hand came down to smash me into the ground. I leaped back and tried to slice at his hand before he could pull it away. It cut away at his flesh, dark shadows pouring out each and every way. As soon as the wound appeared, it disappeared. He simply laughed.

"That scythe will do nothing to me until the lock is on Tartarus. Wounds mean nothing until my defeated body has somewhere to go."

I frowned. I was told that I needed to weaken him first. Could my father and his brothers have been wrong? It wasn't as if there was a time where Tartarus didn't exist, at least as far as Kronos was concerned.

So that meant no one could have known and I would have to keep him entertained until Huntley got the lock. Great.

But at least I knew Huntley was safe and I could hold Kronos off here. I spun the scythe in my hand.

"Well, it's good I could do this all day." I jumped up and sliced at his torso. My eyes widened as I saw what was inside—some of the gods were in his stomach. When the wound opened him up, a few of the gods leaped out.

Kronos grabbed at his wound, trying to push the gods back inside. Those who got out in time ran for it, leaving me to fight Kronos. I couldn't blame them after what they had been through.

Staggering back, Kronos let out a loud scream. Now I realized where he was getting his energy from—it was from the gods inside, not from Tartarus being opened.

That changed everything. I would need to simply aim for his torso and keep letting more and more gods out, careful not to also cut them in half.

It was clear that Kronos knew my plan as he made sure to shield his stomach with his arms as I came for him. I sliced again and again, ripping the shadowy flesh off his arms. It was no use though. He still had a lot of energy to take from gods.

Jumping back, I tried to strategize what to do next. I needed a clear shot, but he was on the complete defensive now, but I had a feeling that wouldn't last long.

And just as I thought that, I watched his hands go up in the sky and come straight down upon me.

CHAPTER 22

Huntley

I didn't know how to feel. I mean, I was really happy he came and rescued me, but I was still pissed at him for drugging Chrys so she couldn't remember who she was, kidnapping her and taking her to some remote island to convince her she was his daughter and that she needed to kill Zeus and then almost getting her killed. Granted, Zeus really wasn't going to stop until he killed her, but how Prometheus went about it wasn't the answer.

But he did just save my ass, so I was going to let it slide for now.

"Thank you for saving me. Think you can help us defeat the last two?"

He licked his lips. "With pleasure. I'm not a fan of these daimons, nor am I a fan of Aether for ratting me out earlier. And the whole taking-over-Olympus thing."

Hermes stood up and joined the two of us. "And here I didn't think you were allowed back into Olympus. Haven't you been in hiding this whole time?"

"I have been. Actually, I wasn't too far from here—one mountain over when I saw the commotion. You are lucky that was where I was hiding."

"You hid this close to Hephaestus? I would think you would want to stay away from all the gods after you did," I commented.

"That's why I picked Hephaestus—under normal circumstances, all the gods leave him alone."

He had a point there. It seemed that none of the gods wanted to be around him. "Well, what gave it away that there was something going on?"

"Oh, you know, the dark sky, Olympus being in ruin, the world being destroyed by one of my brothers. Typical apocalyptic stuff."

It was good to see he still had his humor intact. I grabbed the knives on the ground and handed one to Hermes. Prometheus readied his sword as the two remaining daimons circled above us.

"You killed our brother!" Lupa yelled down at us. "I'll never forgive you for that!"

Prometheus grinned. "Oh yeah? Then come at me."

What I learned today was that daimons were not as smart as I thought they would be. They were really just little balls of badness that thought more of themselves than they should have. I watched as Prometheus sliced Lupa in half, his dead body landing to the side of me. I tried not to vomit, as I had already done so twice today.

Prometheus turned to Achos. "Are you too ready to die?"

Achos came screaming as he flew down at us, but it was all for nothing as Prometheus sliced him in half. Hermes and I didn't have to do a thing.

"Well." Prometheus stepped up to my shirt that was now on the ground. He grabbed it and cleaned his sword with it. "Shall we get to Hephaestus?"

I glared at him. "Did you really have to clean that with my shirt?"

He shrugged. "What? Oh, was this yours? Maybe I just liked looking at your abs, Huntley. It's apparent you've been working out these past two years."

I rolled my eyes as I turned to where we needed to head. Now that Hermes couldn't fly, we would have to walk fast. We were close at least.

Then it occurred to me—how were we going to get back to the underworld quickly? I turned to Hermes.

"Are you going to be able to fly anytime soon?" I asked.

He shook his head. "No. I won't be able to. We are going to have to go back to the entrance and wait for Charon."

I bit my lip. There was no way that was going to be fast enough.

"What's the rush?" Prometheus asked. "I mean, I presumed Hephaestus is making the lock for Tartarus so someone, who I assume is Chrys since Huntley is here and because she is probably the one who let him out, can destroy Kronos."

"Chrys is currently battling Kronos, so time is of the essence," Hermes explained.

He raised an eyebrow. "Before the lock is on Tartarus? Does she have a death wish?"

I gave him a look that said, "I really didn't want to hear that."

Prometheus shrugged. "Look, that would not be how I would have done it. I would have made sure Tartarus was intact before battling him."

"The world is almost destroyed. This is one of the few places that has not been leveled by his wrath. Do you really think the world would have lasted any longer? Besides, she needs to weaken him first. We should get back right on time."

"Fair. I'll accompany you and make sure you get back all right." Prometheus bowed. "I, Prometheus the titan, will be at your disposal."

"Really?" I asked. "That seems unlike you."

"I, dear Huntley, am what created you humans. I do care about you a lot and wouldn't want to see my creation destroyed. Call it kindness, call it vanity, I don't care. I just don't want all of them killed."

I must have skipped that day of history class. I shrugged. "Whatever. Just don't get in our way."

He laughed. "You're welcome for saving your asses."

He had a point there. He had no reason other than to help us get involved. Maybe he really did just want to help. Either way, I was going to keep an eye on him.

We made it to Hephaestus's secret tunnel and ventured down to where the lava was bubbling more than it had the day before. Hephaestus was working away at his bench, hammering something or another.

I coughed really loud. Hephaestus turned and saw

me.

"Huntley, you are back. And I see you brought different friends this time. I am glad."

That was fair—he didn't have the best relationships with the other three I had brought.

"I have. Did you finish the lock?" I asked.

He nodded to his table. "I am almost done. I just have to finish up the last parts. It will be just a few minutes. Feel free to sit down."

I took a seat because I was tired after everything we went through. Hermes took the other seat and leaned his arms on his knees. He appeared to be sweating, and I didn't think it was from the heat.

"You all right?" I asked.

"I'll be fine. Don't worry about me."

Prometheus stepped up to me. "You always make the strangest friends, don't you?"

I shrugged. "I suppose. I don't have all the drama and baggage you each have. You all are new to me, so I don't know whom to keep away from or whom I should trust. But I like to believe I can trust most gods if they seem genuine. But I shouldn't be like that after the stunt you pulled, now should I?"

He laughed. "I suppose not. Many gods use each

other, so when a human believes us, it's quite refreshing, isn't it Hermes? You are quite the trickster yourself. We could really screw over everyone if we worked together."

"Very funny, but I'm not in the mood. We need to get that lock and get out of here," Hermes mumbled. He appeared to be really hurting. We needed to get him to Maka, fast.

"All done!" Hephaestus held up the lock. It shimmered a bluish green, just like the scythe did. "It is made of adamantine, just like the gates are. Once you close the lock over the gate doors, it will not be opened, at least not without—"

"Don't tell me!" I yelled. "I don't want to know."

"That's fair. We don't want this happening again." Hephaestus handed me the lock. It was heavy, just like I expected from watching *X-Men*. At least they got something right.

Now we would just have to get back to the underworld as fast as we could. If only we had some way to get through the waters faster. Then it hit me.

"Hey, Hephaestus, you don't happen to have a spare motor to go on a boat do you?"

CHAPTER 23

Chrys

I didn't get out of the way quick enough, but I was able to use the snath of the scythe and shield to stop his hand from crushing me, but just barely. I had never realized I had this much strength, or perhaps it was all adrenaline.

His hand kept pushing down, sending me sliding back as I held the scythe above my head. If I could just twist the scythe, I could slice his hand and get him to retreat. But he was strong, and it was taking everything I had to keep him from crushing me.

"You are no match for me, Chrysanthemum. You should just give up now and perhaps I'll let you live."

I shook my head. "No, I'll never let you destroy this

world. I love it too much."

"But you aren't even allowed to enjoy it—your domain is in the underworld. Why does it matter if this world or Olympus is destroyed? It wouldn't hurt your world."

I didn't even answer as he was just repeating himself at that point. When would villains ever learn? But his monologue distracted him enough where he let up and I was able to twist the knife and slice his hand. He jerked back, and I made a run for his torso. With a flick of my hand, I was able to slice down upon his stomach.

More gods were able to escape this time as he tumbled down and fell to the ground. He let out a roar.

"Are you finished now?" I said. "If you give up now, well, I wouldn't let you go, I would just make you wait in Tartarus until we locked it."

"Do you really think your dear Huntley will be able to get the lock? Do you not think Aether sent others to stop him?"

I frowned. I didn't think Aether would want to stop me from stopping Kronos since he wanted to rule over all the worlds. Apparently I was wrong. Then I remembered—his offspring were in Tartarus and would be sent back once the gate was locked. It made sense.

Then it occurred to me that if Kronos couldn't be killed, then neither could the daimons. So Huntley wasn't safe.

Part of me wanted to go and help him, but I knew that wasn't a good idea. I would just have to trust him. Huntley would make it—he had Hermes with him. Hermes was strong and would be able to keep the two of them safe. I just knew it.

As the gods jumped out of the wound I had created, I spotted a familiar blond-haired god. I hurried after Apollo and grabbed him.

"Not so fast. You are going to help me—you owe me!"

He turned to me, eyes full of terror. "Are you kidding me? He will kill me or eat me. I don't want to go through that again."

"You'll just be a distraction. I promise no harm will come to you." I raised my scythe. "Or I could just kill you right now. We both know you deserve it."

He let out a sigh. "Fine, what do you want me to do?"

"You are the god of archery. Can you use those to attack him? Distract him for a moment while I get the rest of the gods out? He seems to get weaker and weaker every time I attack him. I think this last one will make him a lot more manageable."

"And then what though? You heard him. If there is no lock, then he won't be sent to Tartarus. Do you really think that human of yours can go against daimons and get back in time?"

I nodded. "I do. He stopped you and Prometheus didn't he? I think he's capable of a lot more than you gods give him credit for. He's the prince of the underworld, after all."

Apollo laughed and rubbed his face with his hands. "You are ridiculous. Both of you. But fine. I'll help. Mainly because I know you are going to kill me if I don't."

"Glad we see eye to eye. Now, if you'll be so kind and start shooting arrows at Kronos's torso. I'll sneak behind him and try to attack that way."

He nodded, and a bow and arrows appeared in his hand. "Well, good luck then."

I began running around Kronos as Apollo started shooting at him as he stood up. Kronos let out another roar as he tried to swipe at Apollo. Before he could make contact, I sliced across his back.

More gods jumped away, and from what I could tell, that was the last of them. I took a deep breath as Kronos turned to face me.

"How dare you! It will all have been for nothing! Tartarus is not yet locked! I'll eat every god alive, and my power will grow more, and no one will stop me, not even some young girl with a stick."

I tightened my grip around the scythe. I could almost hear the primordial voice telling me it was time—that I could give this titan the final blow. Perhaps it was tricking me—perhaps it too wanted to be free of this burden. Or perhaps Uranus wanted to see his son destroyed once and for all.

Kronos swung his hand at me, but I jumped out of the way. I glanced over to find Apollo was long gone now. I couldn't blame him—his job was over. I kept running around Kronos as he swiped and kicked at me. His movements were sluggish—he had lost a lot of energy. Perhaps I really could weaken him and earlier it had all been a bluff. He could heal his wounds but not his energy. Now I could finally end this.

I stopped in front of him, facing the large titan—the titan that once ruled over time and was considered the bringer of destruction—the titan that had tried to kill my father and all his siblings. He needed to go back to Tartarus before this world was no longer repairable.

This had to work. I had to trust Huntley. Enough time had gone by for them to get back.

So I jumped straight up and sliced dead center into his skull.

CHAPTER 24

Huntley

I held up the motorboat engine as we stepped out of the volcano tunnel. "What are the odds?"

Prometheus shook his head. "I created you lot, and I still don't quite understand you."

I laughed but quickly stopped as I watched one of the daimons we had killed earlier fly down with a dagger in his hands. Between Prometheus's holding the lock and my holding the motor, there was no way we were going to be able to jump out of the way.

Which was why Hermes quickly turned his back on the daimon and huddled around Prometheus and me. I screamed as the knife went straight into Hermes's back

—the back that had already been wounded.

A moment later we were in front of the gates to the underworld. If only he had transported us a second earlier—if only I had been paying attention.

I stared at Hermes as he collapsed beside Prometheus and me. How was that daimon not dead? I saw him cut in half. I hurried to Hermes's side.

"Hermes, say something! Get up!"

He didn't move.

Tears ran out of my eyes. "Get up!"

Prometheus handed me the lock. "Can you carry both of these?"

I nodded as he went over and hauled Hermes over his shoulder.

"We need to get going. Come on," Prometheus said as he hurried inside the entrance to the underworld. Lucky for us, Charon was just entering.

"Charon!" I called. "We need a boat, fast!"

With a snap of his fingers, he created a boat for us. I quickly threw the lock inside and fixed the motor in it so we had something fast like Maka had used to get us to the gate the first time.

Prometheus took Hermes over to Charon. I could barely hear their conversation.

"Charon, take Hermes to the castle. I'm sure Hades may have some healers that could help him. Go as quick as you can."

"Righty-O. I haven't seen Hermes this bad in a long time," Charon said as he began paddling. The boats had already been filled with souls and more refugees.

Prometheus jumped into the boat I had souped up. "Let's go!"

I nodded, tears still filling my eyes. I wanted to help Hermes. I wanted to use this boat to take him to Maka as fast as I could, but I knew we had a more important mission to accomplish. Chrys was counting on me—I had to put this lock on the gate of Tartarus.

The boat was fast, and I was afraid we were going to hit a bump and be thrown out of it, so I held on as best as I could. Lucky for me, Maka had taken me through these waters and I knew exactly where to go.

The underworld was still dark but not as bad as when the gates had been opened. The water seemed almost colorless and stale—which was much different from when this place was fully operating. I couldn't wait until it all went back to normal—when everything and everyone would be fine.

Prometheus and I didn't say anything as we raced

through the underworld. He seemed to be glancing around, and I finally realized why—he had never been down here. Most gods and titans hadn't. I was so used to this place I had forgotten they were either banned or simply didn't want to be here.

The more we raced, the more I worried about Hermes. He had to be okay—he just had to be. I couldn't imagine a world without him. He was one of the gods that I considered to be a good friend. He helped Chrys as much as he could—he cared for her more than he cared about his own life.

Which was why he put himself in front of that knife.

I pushed forward. I had to focus. I had to keep going for him. If we failed, then it all would be for nothing.

I prayed that Chrys was fine and that she didn't try to send Kronos down here yet. We had wasted time fighting everyone, so I couldn't be too certain. At least we were able to get this motor.

We were coming upon the gates now, and I knew it would be okay—I knew we would be right on time. We just had to be.

As we rode up, Prometheus and I jumped out. I had the lock in my hand and ran straight toward the gate. Prometheus helped me get it around the chains, and we locked it up.

Then it was like an implosion as all the darkness of the world was sucked up and into Tartarus. The pressure was enormous, and I slammed back into the gate. Darkness engulfed my senses, and I passed out.

CHAPTER 25

Chrys

I had done it. Kronos had been returned to Tartarus.

I stared at the empty air where he once stood. Huntley had made it in time, just as I knew he would.

Collapsing to the ground, I breathed a heavy sigh. I would need to return to the underworld to make sure everything was cleared up and to prepare to attack Aether. I did not want to have to fight again, but I had to do what I had to do.

As I began to stand up, I saw a figure step up to me, clapping. My entire body froze as I watched Aether make his way over to me.

"I commend you, Chrys. I honestly didn't think you

and that dear human husband of yours would succeed in stopping Kronos."

I grabbed the scythe that lay next to me. "Why did you try to stop him from getting the lock?"

"That's simple—I didn't want to see my poor children sent back there. It doesn't matter though; they served their purpose in helping me take over Olympus."

"You would just use your own children like that?"

He stopped, now just out of reach of my scythe. "Yeah. That's their purpose. Besides, it was the price to pay for stopping Kronos. He was really making a mess of things, if you hadn't noticed. Although I had hoped you would have found a way to destroy him completely, but I won't complain. He's out of my hair now."

I shook my head. "How were you able to plan so quickly? I only came to you mere days ago."

"Simple, Chrys. I'm as old as time. I understand how people think, how gods think, and I knew the moment your father died that you would try to open the gate. Then appear to me—needing me to translate that text."

"Was that text correct? Or did you lie to me?"

He smiled. "Oh, I never lie, my dear Chrys. I gave you the exact information that was written on there."

"You could have warned me that Kronos was going

to escape."

"As if you didn't know."

I frowned. He was right—I knew the cost. I just wanted to blame him for everything that had happened. I couldn't, however. I only could blame myself for all this destruction.

"What do you want?"

Aether shrugged. "I just want to finally rule. First it was my brother Uranus, then his son Kronos, then his son Zeus. Enough is enough—someone that can truly lead this world needs to step up."

"And I suppose that's you?"

"Of course. I am one of the oldest beings that are still alive. I deserve it."

"By almost destroying the world?" I asked.

He laughed. "You think all those others who began their leadership didn't do so after a war broke out? Change always brings death—there is no denying that."

I pinched the bridge of my nose. "You know, I'm really sick of you villains just monologuing. Can we just battle now so I don't have to listen to another old dude try to tell me what to do?"

He pulled his white hair back into a ponytail. "Fair enough. I'm sick of young brats not listening to me anyway." He finished up and smiled. "Oh, and I'm sure that your father and everyone forgot to mention…" Aether pulled a sword out that glittered in the sunlight that was now coming out from the darkened clouds above. "There is another weapon made of adamantine."

Which meant it could block my scythe. Great. "They seemed to have forgotten to mention that."

"I have held on to it for centuries, waiting for the right time. It had cost me quite a pretty penny too."

He attacked with the sword, and I used the snath of the scythe to block his sword and swung around to try to cut him in half. He was able to block my attack again.

Aether swung again and again at me. As the sword came crashing down, I blocked with my shield, and it smashed into pieces, sending me flying back with a large cut along my left arm.

I cursed under my breath as he used the opportunity to pounce on me, swinging his sword straight at my face. I blocked it with the scythe. He kept pushing down harder and harder, but I was able to hold him back.

"You know, this almost reminds me when we almost fucked in my opium den. Brings back good times, doesn't it?" He grinned at me.

I used my legs to kick him straight in the torso, sending him backward. He brushed himself off and smiled.

"You've a lot of spunk, Chrys. It is no wonder Huntley likes you so much."

I glared at him as we began to circle around. "Why are you so focused on him? It's kind of creepy."

"I just see so much potential in him, and I want to crush it. You know that's why he died, right? From the poison I created. If it weren't for his friends, he would still be in my den, dreaming the days away."

"What are you talking about?"

"Oh, that's right, you two probably never talked about it. Huntley followed you to my place, and I kidnapped him and gave him some of my special drugs. If it weren't for Hermes and those others, he would have been trapped forever, just like every other human."

I screamed as I attacked him, slicing with my scythe again and again. He stepped out of the way for each and every attack, laughing at my anger. He didn't even use his sword to block, as he was quick.

And then, before I knew it, he stabbed straight into

my stomach, grinning.

CHAPTER 26

Huntley

When I opened my eyes, I found Pothos and Hades standing over me. I sat up real quick and almost fell back over from dizziness. I held my head.

"Careful." Pothos held out his hand. "You hit your head on the gate and passed out. At least that's what Prometheus said…"

Right. Prometheus. I glanced around to find him sitting in a chair near the wall. He had brought me back here? Perhaps he wasn't a bad guy after all.

"Mel hasn't killed him yet?" I asked.

Pothos laughed. "Really, that's the first thing you say? Well, I don't blame you for what we have been through. She tried, but we stopped her."

I glanced around some more, looking for a face in the room. I didn't see any sign of him. "Where is Hermes?"

Pothos frowned and glanced over to Hades.

Hades answered. "He didn't make it. But his soul is at rest in Elysium Fields. He will forever be in paradise."

"Now tell him the bad news," Zeus said from the corner of the room. He was standing next to Pothos.

Hades shot him a look and turned back to me. "What Zeus is trying to say is that you did a good job putting the lock back. Tartarus is closed, and now the souls are returning there."

I knew what he was trying to say. "So all three of your souls are trying to return too, aren't they?"

He nodded. "Unfortunately, yes. We are trying to hold on as much as possible, but it's getting harder every second."

I peered around again. "Where is Chrys? Did she succeed?"

"She did. Kronos is back where he belongs. As to where she is… She isn't back yet."

I stood up. "We have to go get her. What if Aether attacked? He attacked us already with his daimons—he will probably be watching and waiting for when she is the weakest. We have to go help her."

Hades grabbed my shoulder. "You are no match for Aether. You aren't going out there."

"Yes, I am!" I shouted back.

"No you are not! If you die, then my daughter will have nothing! You can't leave!"

Hades was angrier than I had ever imagined him. I understood his fear, but I couldn't just stand here while my wife was battling for her life. "She can't battle Aether alone! We need to send reinforcements!"

"We are, Huntley. We are. But there aren't many gods left who can fight. Even less who are willing…"

"What about you three?" I nodded to Zeus and Poseidon. "If you three are already going to die, why don't you go up there and help her?"

"Because we'll be sent to Tartarus even quicker," Zeus answered. "We are biding our time here."

I shook my head and headed toward the door. "Then I'll fight with her."

"I said no, Huntley! I'll figure out something."

"We don't have time! We have to go now!" I yelled back.

Hades grabbed me by the wrist. I turned to face him,

and that was when a fist came straight at my face and knocked my lights out.

CHAPTER 27

Chrys

I collapsed to the ground, blood pouring out of my stomach. Aether swiped his leg and kicked me straight in the head.

"I know your weakness, Chrys. It's the human. You know how many gods have fallen because of some human? It's pathetic."

"I bet you don't even know the meaning of love," I spat out. Blood trickled down my mouth. I needed to use the herbs and fast.

The only problem was, Aether wasn't going to drag this out.

He stood above me and jabbed the sword down

straight at my face. I rolled out of the way, trying to guard myself against him and spot where I had dropped the scythe. It was a couple of meters to the other side of him.

Aether's sword came down on me again and again, trying to cut me up in a million pieces. I was able to roll out of the way each time, but I could feel my wound aching more and more. Everything began to blur. I reached out for the scythe when I felt something crush my hand. I let out a scream as Aether's boot came down on my fingers.

He leaned down to my face, his foot still on my hand. "Well, it seems you weren't strong enough in the end to take me down. This is your last chance." He traced his finger along my cheek. "Join me or die."

I spat straight in his face.

He frowned. "Suit yourself!"

I closed my eyes as he was about to stab me straight in the throat. Suddenly a loud explosion rocked the earth around me and even with my eyes closed, I saw a flash of light. As I opened my eyes, I found Aether on his back, struggling to get up.

"What the—" I began as a figure stepped before me. It was my father holding his trident.

"Father. What are you doing here?" I tried to get up. I grimaced.

He knelt by my side. "Careful. Do you have the herbs that Circe gave you?"

I nodded as I reached in my pocket and pulled them out. I placed them on the wound and could already feel the wound close. I took a deep breath and let it out slowly.

Aether stood up as two more figures stepped beside me. It was Zeus and Poseidon. I gave them both looks, not sure if it was a good thing they were on my side or not. I supposed I needed help either way.

Laughing, Aether snapped his fingers. Figures began to come out from the cloud layer and down from Olympus. It was the gods he turned. I spotted Artemis and Athena.

"There's too many of them," I whispered. "I don't want to use my scythe on them—they don't deserve it."

Father patted my back. "Don't worry about them. We have your back. Just destroy Aether as quickly as possible so that this battle doesn't have to end in too many deaths."

I turned to find dozens of gods armed and ready to fight. I couldn't believe my eyes. Had this many gods actually come to help me? I mean, really they were fighting for their lives too, but still. I hadn't had so many people on my side before.

War broke out as the gods descended upon us. I ducked as Artemis came straight for me. She really could hold a grudge. She tried to stab me with her sword when Poseidon blocked her.

"Hey there, beautiful. How about you dance with me for a while?"

Ew. I felt bad for Artemis as she began to fight him. I was sort of rooting for her even though I knew I needed to be against Aether.

Aether stood up, and the two of us faced each other —ready to fight to the death. My wounds had healed, and I was ready for him. Everyone had my back even if I was the only one who could defeat him. If the time came, they could help me.

We circled each other, both at the center of the battle that was going on all around us. Aether laughed.

"Pathetic, isn't it? They're all friends and lovers until a war breaks out. Then it's all for one."

"Only because you turned them to your side."

"Did I though? I only showed that I was powerful, and smart people follow powerful people. It's only natural."

"You'll pay the price for everything you caused. All of this would have been over if it weren't for you."

He laughed. "Oh, I have only begun."

Aether swung the sword at me and it clashed against the snath of my scythe. Sparks flew as he swung again and again, and I blocked it each and every time. He stepped back, giving me enough time to swing my scythe.

The ground shook as he jumped out of the way, and a large chasm was unleashed. Gods moved away quickly as they saw the earth rupture.

The sword came straight at my face, and I bent backward, almost falling over. I swept the scythe under Aether's legs, but he jumped out of the way. My arms grew tired from wielding the scythe, but I couldn't give up now.

Around us, gods fought for their lives—wanting their life back to normal, if normal was even reachable at this point. I saw my mother in the distance, using her power over plants to defeat Athena.

At least, I thought she was winning.

I watched as Athena's sword went straight into my mother's stomach. I let out a scream. I could hear my own father screaming as well on the other side of the battlefield.

"You should be more careful not to turn your attention away from your own opponent."

Before I could swing the scythe and block Aether's attack, his sword came down and smacked me on the side of the head.

I hit the ground, rolling across the dirt. I had let go of the scythe, and it was too far away to reach before Aether was upon me.

"Goodbye, Chrys. It was a pleasure." Aether raised his sword when vines came from the ground and wrapped around Aether's wrists and ankles. He couldn't move.

Before I could think twice about what was going on, I crawled over to grab my scythe, and with one movement of my arm, I sliced his head off.

Aether's head rolled on the ground before me, blood pooling around his body. The vines fell to the ground. I realized who it was that used them.

I turned to find my mother, holding her arms out— her stomach covered in blood. As if it were her dying wish that I survived, she collapsed to the ground.

"Mother!" I screamed as I raced over to her. The

battle had paused—realizing that their leader had been killed and there was no reason to fight anymore. I knelt by my mother, grabbing her cold hand.

"Please! Don't leave me! Mother!"

It was too late—she was gone. I didn't even get to say goodbye. I didn't get to tell her that I forgave her and that I regretted not spending more time with her. Our relationship had always been rocky, but I never wanted this to happen—I never imagined this would happen. I didn't think she could ever die because she was never strong enough to go to battle. Apparently, I was wrong. She was more of a bad ass than I gave her credit for.

Tears dripped down my face and onto her cold skin. This couldn't be happening—I had risked everything and now my mother was dead. I tried to reach out with my powers to bring her back but it was too late. I couldn't do anything. I was too weak after the battle now.

Hades made his way through the gods, who simply stood and stared at me. My father knelt beside my mother and closed her eyelids for her. His eyes didn't seem teary but almost understanding, as if he knew it would be her time to go. I didn't understand how he wasn't full of tears next to me. He turned to me and wrapped his arms around me.

"It's all right. She is in Elysium Fields. She is in a better place."

I knew he was right—I knew I could go see her since I was the ruler of the underworld, but that wasn't the same—that wasn't us getting to go shop together somewhere or hang out. I had missed my chance to spend time with her over the past two years, and I couldn't do anything to make up for that.

My father backed away, grabbing his chest. I stared at him. I knew exactly what was happening.

"No, you can't go back! You can't go back to Tartarus!" I exclaimed. I could see it now—the string that led down into the underworld and back into the darkness. Just as Circe said, nothing could sever that string.

He placed his hand on my cheek. "It is all right. You stopped Kronos and Aether. I am proud of you, okay? Don't worry about me."

Tears were running down the side of my cheeks. "No! You don't deserve this! I have to be able to do something!"

He shook his head as Poseidon and Zeus stepped up behind him. They both had the same dark thread tied to them. I kept shaking my head.

"No! No! No!"

Their bodies began to fade when I heard a dark whisper next to me. I stared at the scythe.

"You can cut those ties. Listen to me and never destroy me. Let me be a part of your power—the power of destruction."

Without hesitation, I grabbed the scythe and swung at the threads only I could see.

CHAPTER 28

Huntley

When I woke, I found Chrys standing above me. I quickly wrapped my arms around her.

"Thank goodness you are all right," I said as I squeezed her tight.

"Likewise. I don't know what I would have done if you had gotten hurt."

I released her and examined her. Her clothes were cut and covered in blood, but it appeared that the wounds she had, for the most part, were healed. I glanced around and found Pothos there. As for the other gods, they were all gone.

"What happened? Besides defeating Aether, I mean. I

assume he's dead."

She nodded. "He is." Chrys began crying. "They're gone. It's all my fault. My father and mother are gone."

My eyes widened. I knew Hades would be sent back to Tartarus, but Persephone? I couldn't believe that. Did she go up and battle? Did they all go up and battle and that was why no one was down here?

Then it hit me—this was why Hades didn't want me to battle. If anything happened to me, then Chrys would have been suffering even more. I wrapped my arms around her and let her cry for as long as she wanted.

After about an hour of crying, Chrys and Pothos recapped what happened. Apparently the gods appeared in the nick of time and helped Chrys battle. Persephone was stabbed by Athena, and Aether took the opportunity to try to kill Chrys. Persephone used the last of her strength to stop Aether, and Chrys was able to kill him. After that, Persephone perished and Hades and the others were being drawn back to Tartarus.

Which was when Chrys used the scythe to cut the ties.

Now, apparently, all the gods who died in battle, along with Hades, Zeus, and Poseidon, were in

Elysium. While this sounded like good news to me, there apparently was a catch. Although the ruler of the underworld could visit Asphodel Fields and Elysium, it was heartbreaking to see the ones you loved had forgotten you. Their souls go through the river of Lethe so that they may no longer remember their lives and can rest in peace.

But Chrys was still happy that her father was not suffering in Tartarus, but she still felt guilty that she had caused his death and many of the other gods' deaths as well. Pothos and I had to tell her about Hermes, and that was a painful experience as well.

A few days had passed, and most of the gods had returned to either Olympus or helped to rebuild earth, even Pothos eventually with both of his brothers. There were still many humans left on earth, but the gods needed help to restore the lands so that they could once again be prosperous and whatnot. We took the time to heal and straighten out the underworld, as it was still a mess. I mostly did whatever Chrys ordered me to do, which was mainly contact other gods that resided there and give them tasks.

Chrys and I ventured up to the earth, and I stared out at the giant chasm that had been left by Chrys. It was as large as the Grand Canyon.

"Damn, girl, you should have held back some," I said.

She laughed. "This actually wasn't from the fight—it was from when I severed the ties Father and the others had to Tartarus."

I whistled as I peered down. "Well, it must have worked."

"It did, but it almost came at the cost of the world. The scythe tried to overpower me to destroy everything, but I was able to stop. Eventually."

"It wouldn't be the first time you almost destroyed the entire world with your power."

She laughed. "Hopefully it's the last though."

Chrys knelt down and placed her hands on the ground. It was still dark and ash-like, as this area hadn't been cleaned up by the gods. She closed her eyes and focused. I watched as the dead ground began to turn green with grass and wildflowers. Birds and small creatures began to appear, and Chrys summoned more and more life to this area.

Before I knew it, everything was back to life and this area no longer looked like a wasteland but a place of paradise. With death brought new life, and I was beginning to understand the cycle of this world. I knew now that everything would be all right and we would finally be at peace. At least for a while.

CHAPTER 29

Chrys

I paddled my way through Lethe, the river of lost memories, alone. Huntley understood I didn't want him to come with me, and I stole this boat from Charon, as I didn't need his commentary. I knew this was a mistake, but I had to do it anyway.

In the distance was a beautiful place of life and beauty—a place that not even the most creative mind could dream of. It was the Elysium Fields, and it shone a beautiful green—just like the rolling hills of the alpine meadows.

I grew closer and finally made it to the docks. I stepped onto the creaky boards and made my way into this place that was only meant for the gods.

It appeared like earth, but something about it was more magical and more perfect than earth ever could be. I passed by god after god, some I recognized and many I did not. They all were smiling and in perfect bliss.

I found him, sitting under a white poplar tree. He was at a small table across from Zeus, playing a game of petteia. The black and white stones littered the board as they concentrated on the game. I smiled, seeing my father smiling and enjoying his time.

Behind him was my mother, laying in the grass, staring up at Oceanus as it shimmered. Next to her also laying in the grass was Hermes. I smiled.

They were all fine. They were all happy. That was all I needed to know.

As I turned away, I heard my father's voice call, "Where are you going, my flower?"

Tears filled my eyes as I turned to face him. He smiled at me as he stood and opened his arms. I ran to him and wrapped my arms around him.

"How do you remember? Did you not take the Lethe?"

"How would I forget my only daughter?" he

whispered.

We stood there for a while, gods gathering around us, not sure what was going on or who I was. None of the others seemed to remember, but that didn't matter—I now knew they were all fine and I was able to hear my father call me his flower one last time.

Thank you so much for reading! Readers like you make it possible for authors like me to write stories! If you could spare a moment and leave a review on Amazon, Goodreads, BookBub, and wherever you like to buy books, that would mean the world to me! It really helps authors like me to succeed in the publishing world.

A big thank you again for your patronage. I hope you will check out my other work!

I want to thank everyone who made this novel possible. A big thank you to my editor Justin and Annie who hopefully hasn't gotten sick of reading my stories yet. Thank you to Biserka Design for the amazing covers for this series! I love them lot! A special thank you to Dr. Almira Poudrier at ASU for answering my questions about Greek Mythology as things get weird and confusing and even more weird. And, lastly, thank you to my husband and parents who are always supporting me.

Dani Hoots is a young adult sci-fi and fantasy author and she likes to be inspired by ancient tales. She has a B.S. in Anthropology from Arizona State University, a Masters of Urban and Environmental Planning from ASU, a B.S. in Herbal Science from Bastyr University, and has a non-credited certificate in Sci-fi and Fantasy Writing. She enjoys reading about history, astronomy, and plants and in her spare time she is either watching anime, reading manga, or drawing.

Be sure to check out her YouTube Channel "Mythology & Folklore w/ Dani Hoots" where she discusses different figures and events in mythology. She also has a Patreon that includes a plethora of perks.

Youtube.com/DaniHoots
Patreon.com/DaniHootsAuthor